MAN ON THE OTHER END

Grey Liliy

BROKEN POCKET

ISBN-13: 978-1943161010
ISBN-10: 1943161011

Cover by Grey Liliy

CHAPTER 1

"OH, MAN! YOU took him for broke!" Kirk said, rolling his chair across the wooden floorboards to get a better peek over Ross' shoulder. He stretched half out of his seat, adoring what he saw on the glowing screen past Ross' brown hair and fat shoulders. Lean and blond, Kirk thought he cut the better figure, but nothing was as pretty as the cleared commands blinking back to them on Ross' monitor.

Kirk bit the edge of his thumb as his grin grew wider and wider. Their latest malware masterpiece, *FlowerMantis69*, had infected over six hundred computers since its release last night. Only thirty or so of their backdoor explorations came up with any useful data, but those were the breaks. If you wanted the needle, you had to sort through the haystack. Even with the few chunks of useful data they mined, Kirk and Ross had been conservative with their spoils. They took small amounts of cash from each to keep their malware from being discovered too early, naturally, but their latest snare was too good to pass up.

"He's a total moron, am I right?" Ross asked, chubby fingers tapping away at the keyboard bringing up screens of data to well timed clicks and clacks.

Each folder and browser that popped up on the remote access screen confirmed it: Their idiot victim had used the same password for all of his accounts. Not only that, but it had been stored in a text file on his desktop called "Passwords." At first Ross thought it was a dummy file as a joke, but nope! Completely legitimate. Bank, social media, money handlers, and email alike were all on this tiny text document; a thought out list of site names and addresses complete with a single password.

The same seven letter, one capital, one number password: *Samisno1*.

Ross hadn't been able to help himself, as Kirk said, and he took the guy for broke. When people made it that easy, how could he be blamed? A fool and his money were easily parted, and only a fool protected his investments with that lousy of security. Ross scavenged from every account he could find in the sap's browser history, raking in every last penny from the loser's checking and savings account, followed by the *pièce de résistance*: plastering spam and obscenities all over the man's social accounts.

Not that it mattered. The guy had next to no friends or followers, the most being three or four, and maybe a single 'hello' post on each account. Covering the account with profanities had almost been boring when there would be no one to see the results. Ross figured a friend set the accounts up, so maybe at least one person would get a surprise, assuming even that guy still looked at the things he set up for the imbecile.

Kirk shook Ross' shoulder with a wide grin, rubbing the corner of his eyes in the dim light. From the potato dumplings he'd gotten off his neighbors that morning, to working over an idiot? It shaped out to be a beautiful night. Kirk rolled back to his own computer, pulling up their bank account as he bit a piece of poppy-seed roll they'd got from the market. He grinned as the money transfer showed up as 'pending' in his offshore account. "Nice."

Ross sat back, satisfied. Who said crime didn't pay? And this was so much more profitable than lifting goods or pickpocketing when these fools practically handed Kirk and Ross their money. And they were never going to get caught! Ross swirled around once in the rolling chair, head back against the headrest and feet spread out. "I didn't mean to go that far, but some of these losers make it so easy."

"Going for the final finish?" Kirk asked, flicking the mouse on his desk. Their little Mantis had two end games: a quick getaway that activated on its own after a set time of twenty-four hours that erased itself from the had drive, or what they affectionately dubbed "Devouring the Husband." Kirk hoped for the latter this time around. He bit his lip as his blood rushed just thinking about it, and knowing if anyone deserved it, it was this guy.

Ross kept an eye on Kirk's spreading grin, and for once he could feel his buddy's sadistic spree spreading. "Yeah, why not? Morons that use the same password for everything don't deserve to own a computer."

Ross entered a few commands in the terminal, activating the

"Husband" command hidden in their program. Seconds later, the program sprung to life far away from the two programmers. They no longer had access to the feed, but they didn't need to see it to know that it ate away at everything on the drive, before a final reformat command wiped itself and anything else remaining off the host machine. Not even the operating system was safe from their Mantis. Ross and Kirk closed the command window for the recently deceased machine and pulled up the list of other potentials victims.

Ross scrolled down the list, eyeing the computers. He clicked through a potential and grinned back at Kirk. "Looks like we got a few more idiots."

"Shall we?" Kirk pushed back to his own station. He laced his fingers together, rolling his hands out to stretch the digits. This was only the beginning. They had plans for their Mantis family, and these idiots were just the stepping stones.

CHAPTER 2

RUSSELL HOPKINS' COMPUTER screen was black.

He set his coffee mug on the desk, and let his stack of work papers clatter next to it as he dropped the folder on the surface. Situated in the corner of his bedroom, the computer rested on a small triangular shaped desk that came furnished with the apartment. A fine layer of dust lined the top of the computer box, save for finger-shaped smudges here or there where he had wiped it away waiting for something to load while the machine clicked.

The rest of his room was as tidy and sparse as Russell. A queen sized bed with plain covers, white and sterile, sat up against the wall in the center of the room. A wooden clothes chest was located at the footboard, containing nearly his entire wardrobe of five pairs of pants, and six plain shirts. A decedent black suit, and a grey 'Sunday Suit' hung on the bathroom door in a coal-grey garment bag. Russell's two pairs of shoes were aligned neatly along the left side of the bed. His walls contained a few shelves covered with sparse knick-knack of little value. All of them gifts of some form or another. His entire apartment, sans computer, could fit in the chest at the end of his bed.

Granted, that did nothing to explain the tiny white line blinking in the corner of an otherwise darkened screen.

"Why is it?" Russell said to himself, tapping the side of his thin monitor with the edges of his fingers. It did nothing, so he clicked the power button on the tall box behind it. Russell listened to the machine wind down, and clicked it on again after it grew quiet. Nine out of ten times he could solve his computer woes by doing this ritual. Russell moved his stack of papers to the bed as it booted, and after a few moments, the same blank screen popped up.

Russell typed in a few random keys on the line and hit "Enter." A small line of text that read "Error; invalid command" showed up, but nothing else happened. Russell heaved, his muscles tightening as he felt the stirrings of anger form in his chest. This is why he preferred mechanics to computing. The only automated things he wanted to deal with were transportation related or his gun. In other words, things that required a human element to do what they were built for. Pull the trigger, turn the engine key. These computers practically ran themselves, running far faster than Russell could ever keep up.

He picked up his cell phone and dialed Sam, the one who had insisted Russell own on of these things in the first place. He tapped his finger on the desk as he waited for the other man to answer. Sam had brought him the computer and installed its software one afternoon when they were slow on business without so much as a warning that he was going to do so. Russell had watched him, wary of the thing invading his home as Sam had invited himself in (as he was often known to do).

"You have to catch up with the times, Russ," Sam had said while installing the machine's operating system. Sam rocked back and forth in Russell's chair as the little install line moved across the screen. "I'll even set it up so you can check your bank accounts and stuff. It'll make things easier and we can stop dealing everything in cash, you know?"

Russell eventually warmed up to the machine, as much as he hated to admit. Sam even set up some accounts he could use to see what his co-workers were up to in their free time, which was oddly thoughtful for Russell's odd partner. He never posted anything on them, but Sam and the others would occasionally leave him private messages that they knew Russell read, even if he didn't reply. His boss copied him on emails sent to Sam, for his record, and Russell discovered online coupons through the same venue. He could even check his bank account status without scaring the bank tellers when he walked in the door—always a plus.

Sam knew a lot about computers, and he's the one who brought it to Russell's home, so he should help fix this. Russell clicked the phone off, and re-dialed. He hoped Sam wasn't busy with a woman or bothering their co-workers again. Listening to his partner try and hold a conversation over the phone during intercourse was only something he could tolerate once a week. Russell straightened in his seat when the connection went through, crossing his fingers only one voice answered.

7

"Hey, Russ! What's up? Get a pop up window stuck on your screen again?" Sam asked without preamble. It was eight o'clock, which was Russell's designated "check my e-mail" time. Russell'd been adventurous lately looking at News websites, Sam knew, but the poor guy still had trouble with just basic operations of the computer. Sam considered it pretty safe to say that if Russell was calling at eight, it was computer related. "I told you not to turn off that malware protection I installed."

"Sam," Russell said, voice heavy with aggravation. He pushed at the mouse on his desk, sending it across the mousepad decorated in dull grey. He could feel his face redden in embarrassment. "I did nothing. Machine will not start, and white line blinks at me. Everything is black. What is wrong?"

"Huh," Sam said. Well, he knew the hard drive hadn't failed, the machine was too new and he hadn't been having problems before now. Sam knew what this sounded like, but that didn't seem quite right either. Russell was hopeless, but Sam doubted he could manage reformatting a hard drive on his own. That required actually visiting a settings menu, and the man had barely come to terms with icons on his desktop. Sam tapped his fingers on his knee. *Malware, maybe?* "This sounds a bit over my head, actually."

"So you can't help?" Russell asked.

"No, but I do know someone who can." Sam pulled up his contact registry on his own laptop. He scanned down the list for the best guy he knew for the job. Well, the only person he knew for the job. Sam needed more techie friends for these situations, but not everyone was willing to put up with Sam's needs and unique personality. He pulled up the number, and bit his lip at the matching photograph staring back. Sam crossed his fingers. "Fair warning though, the guy's not in the uh, business, if you know what I mean. So he might be a little jumpy around you, bud. You think you can handle playing nice?"

Russell sighed into the phone. Working with civilians came easy to Sam and the others, but Russell was still awkward around them. Even the people at the grocery store stared at him as he carried his basket, minding his own business. He was too tall, too muscled, too—as a small girl once put it: "Scary looking." But Russell could do this. He could avoid scaring Sam's friend and get his computer fixed.

Russell steeled himself sitting up straighter in his seat. "I will be fine. I will be good host."

Sam bit his lip, hoping that was true. He really couldn't afford to lose his one tech connection. Then who would fix his servers? Porn sites didn't run themselves! "Great, I'll give him a call tonight, and I bet he'll be there tomorrow."

"Thank you," Russell said. He clicked the phone off and glanced around his apartment.

He needed to clean if company was coming.

Alfred "Alfie" Knight stumbled along the sidewalk, struggling to walk straight as he searched through his carrier bag for Sam's business card. Alfie'd been warned he'd need it to prove who he was, if that didn't just make his morning. Sam's friend was the suspicious type, apparently. Alfie found the card in the bottom of the side pocket, and heaved his bag strap higher on his shoulder. His sneakers tread down the cobblestone street, and the bumpy walk had him repeatedly shoving his glasses back up on his nose. This apartment complex was seriously lacking in the parking department when the nearest parking garage was a good six blocks away.

Alfie spotted the ten story Mediterranean style complex on the next block, and picked up his pace to cross the street before the signal could change. He entered the main door, whistling at the carved grapes in the doorframe, jogging over to the elevator to catch it before it left the floor. The complex patterned tile work under his feet with their matching wall trimmings sang of the craftsmanship that set them into place. The earth-toned patterns made everything a treat of straight lines and squares, that still felt rustic and homey.

Sam's friend ain't bad off, Alfie thought to himself as he trotted out of the elevator on the sixth floor. Alfie checked the back of the card again for the room number he'd scribbled down after Sam's phone call: 6-67D. He found the appropriate brown door at the end of an outcrop in the hallway, and knocked with a light rap.

Alfie was five foot six inches with about one hundred and sixty pounds on him. He had scraggly brown hair that fell around his neck, and stylish wire-frame glasses he only wore on business excursions. It made people think he was smarter or older depending on the client, which meant they were much more likely to cooperate. Sad, but true. He saved his contacts for special nights, which included the ones where he wasn't wearing a green polo shirt and khaki slacks. Alfie considered himself an all around average fellow, not too slight or too tall.

The man who answered the door was a monster. Sam hadn't mentioned that part when he called Alfie about the job.

Alfie's grip on his carrier bag tightened. He could feel his blood start a marathon race at the same time his feet glued themselves to the floor. The man standing in the artificially faded doorway had to be a body builder, or some sort of special service military man. Alfie was too terrified to think of any other options that would explain that physique.

Russell Hopkins stood six feet and some easy. The man's muscles were large enough to be intimidating, but not so much that they would hinder the man's movements. There was definitely no hiding them under the white tank top and straight legged blue jeans that fit snugly on his form. Even the bare feet sticking out from under his jeans were sturdy. Hopkins looked like he could crush Alfie by breathing on him. His piercing blue eyes were focused and a tad crazed, easily visible with his blond hair perfectly combed in a side part.

"H-hello," Alfie said. He was cat cornered by a doberman. Every inch of Alfie's body told him to sprint down the hallway and never come back. Except for his brain, which reminded him that it was his friend Sam who recommended his help, and he wasn't in a position to turn down new clients. Even the talented could have trouble making money when you tried to stay out of the government's service or illegal side of things. Alfie didn't have much patience for tech companies or partnerships, either. So that left him with basic computer repair for his income.

Alfie forced a pleasant smile, holding Sam's business card up in plain sight. "Are you Sam's friend, Russell Hopkins?"

"Yes," Russell said. He held his hand out to shake the other man's hand. The small guest stared at it and made no move to take the extended limb. Russell shifted his weight, his hand still holding out in the middle of the air. *Shaking was friendly, right?* Russell had promised Sam he wouldn't scare this one. The poor man still looked skittish and ready to bolt. He dropped his hand back to his side. "Russell Hopkins. Sam did not say your name."

"Alfred Knight, sir." Alfie nearly smacked himself. *Why did he add the 'sir!?'* Alfie fought the grimace that wanted to cover his face. He beat it down with a lick lip and another forced smile. "But most people just call me 'Alfie.'"

"Alfie," Russell repeated, scrunching his face at the childish nickname.

Not one he would have picked. If anything, the young man at his door looked more like an "Al," but Russell wasn't one to judge. It was always safer in the long run to pick your own nickname than to let someone else do it. Russell took a step back to let the man into his apartment. "This way."

Alfie forced one foot in front of the other. The man's voice intimidated as much as his muscles, spoken in this relaxed, calculated tone that could either be ignorance or patience. Alfie hoped for the latter as he squeezed by the large man and into the single-room apartment. From the colorful tiled hallway, to bare white walls and trim, Hopkins' room was an exercise in opposites. The place looked un-lived in; sterile. Terrified to touch anything, Alfie stood deathly still a few feet from the door. Compared to his home covered in computer wires, old equipment, and cabling sprawled everywhere, this was a wasteland of white. Alfie sighed in relief when he spotted the computer in the corner.

Home territory.

"May I?" Alfie asked, pointing at the machine, "or would you like to start it up?"

Russell sat on the bed, parallel to the computer desk. He set his hands on his knees, and tried to relax his shoulders. "Do what you need. I watch."

"Sounds good," Alfie said. He sat in the four-legged, non-rolling, desk chair, feeling as stiff as the wood it was made from. He pulled his laptop out from the bag and set it on the side so it'd be ready to go if he needed it. Alfie's fingers fell in place on the keyboard, and the tightness in his limbs loosened with their familiarity. As long as he concentrated on the machine and not the beast next to him, he'd be fine. "Now let's see what we've got."

Alfie started the computer up, and encountered the main screen. He entered in his first command, and frowned when the information came back on the next line. Alfie already knew the problem, but he tried a few more times to be sure. Finally, he pulled up the listing of the hard drive's stats.

"Your drive's been reformatted down to the firmware," Alfie said. As Mr. Hopkins stared blankly at him, he realized Sam hadn't been exaggerating when he said the man was not friendly with Alfie's lifeblood. "That means it's been erased, sort of. What did you do the last time you were on the machine?"

"Last night, I check e-mail. I visit site Sam send me. After I finish, I locked the machine like Sam showed me from the menu." Russell shifted on the bed, head low. "Nothing else. Yesterday night, I start machine, and that screen show up."

Alfie tapped his fingers on the keyboard. Knowing Sam, he had a good idea what happened to Hopkins' computer, and just where it came from. "What site did you visit? Were there any pop-ups or ads?"

"Some joke site, and yes there were pop-ups. I closed them."

"Okay," Alfie turned and opened up his laptop, pulling up his favorite program. He connected the two machines together with a cord he pulled from his bag. There was nothing more fun than seeing data that had been deleted. He'd find out what happened in no time. In the meanwhile, however, Alfie had a few suspicions that they might want to deal with now. "Mr. Hopkins?"

"Russell."

"Right, Russell, can you do me a favor?" Alfie asked. He loaded his software and started to run through the files still hidden on the drive. *Yeah, not good.*

"What can I do?" Russell asked. The smaller man shoved his glasses up on his face, looking at his laptop warily. His entire demeanor had shifted from a skittish little pup, to a professional in his element. Russell could appreciate that.

"Now, don't be too worried yet, this is just a precaution," Alfie said. He frowned at the last log file he found on the machine. "But you might want to call your bank. It looks like you got hit with some nasty malware, and while I don't know exactly what it is yet, it'd be a good idea to make sure nothing happened to your accounts as soon as possible. I'll help you reset your passwords on the rest of your sites as well as soon as I restore your hard drive."

Russell stood from the bed and did as he was told as his guest tuned him out to type furiously on his laptop.

"Thank you," Russell said. He flipped his phone closed, and clutched it in his hand.

At the telltale sign of smashed electronics, Alfie jumped halfway out of the desk chair. Bits of crushed cell phone spilled out between Russell's fingers, littering the floor in green circuits and black plastic. Russell stood stone still as a statue, save for the slight trembling of his hand pulsing around the main body of the crushed phone.

Alfie's hand shook as he shoved his glasses back on his face. The wire frame clicked together, rattling the nosepiece. "I take it money's missing?"

"You said 'malware,' yes? What is this?" Russell opened his fist, turning his palm so the remainder of his phone cluttered to the ground in a pile. He used his thumb to brush off the few sharp edges that embedded themselves in his skin. The mess mocked him, ruining his clean floor, with a guest not two feet away no less! Russell went to his closet to fetch a broom. "And how does lead to my money being gone?"

"Malware is a computer program that does malicious things to your computer," Alfie said, hands crawling back to the keyboard and mouse as he inched back into the chair. He forced his breathing to calm. Business. Everything would be okay if he concentrated on the machine, and not the madman smashing electronics. "Most people just call it a computer virus, even though they're not quite the same thing."

Alfie flipped through the recovered files as they listed on his laptop screen. He could restore the man's machine, but it would take a while to reset all of his passwords and update his account protections like Alfie had offered. He wasn't getting paid for that part, but common decency wouldn't allow him to let the guy's computer stay this compromised.

Alfie frowned at the file on Russell's desktop listing all of his account addresses and the password used to open it. *Samisno1*. Alfie rubbed between his eyes, and closed the file with a determined click. The next time Sam needed his servers worked on, Alfie was charging double. He also made a note to update Russell's anti-malware software. From the looks of it, Sam went to the trouble of installing one, but forgot turn on automatic updates.

Alfie moved on until he got to the infected files, but didn't recognize the malware immediately. *New one.* He opened the command windows and frowned at the complex coding. Alfie went back to the main file list and started to segregate out document files. He'd have to reinstall to get rid of this nightmare.

Alfie glanced at Russell out of the corner of his eye as he typed. "You got hit with a nasty one I haven't seen before. It gave the person behind it a backdoor to your computer, so they could control it remotely. The short version of what you want to know is they used that back door to get into your bank account through your online account."

"So person did this, yes?" Russell said, sweeping up the last of his damaged cell phone. He looked over Alfie's shoulder at the mass of text and numbers on his screen, scrolling by faster than he could read. Russell fingers twitched on the broom handle. "Not machine by itself?"

"More or less, but I'd make a bet the malware that let them into your machine was loaded automatically from an ad somewhere. I doubt you were personally targeted." Alfie pointed at the tray full of parts Russell was still holding in his hand. He was a big buff guy, and still very terrifying, but the confusion in his eyes did wonders for making Alfie feel bad for him. That was more calming than anything else about this situation. "If I were you, I'd find another phone and call your bank back. Explain what happened, and then I'd file a police report."

Russell dumped the parts in a trash bin. He clipped the ashtray back to the broom and set it against the wall. "This will find them?"

"Doubtful," Alfie made a copy of the man's logs and registries. He pulled out a secure thumb drive, and copied over what he could find of the malware. He may not work officially for any tech companies, but they should at least be informed of what was floating around so their anti-malware programs could be updated as soon as possible. "But it should get you your money back from insurance or a fraud report at the very least."

"Is possible to find these people?" Russell asked, flexing his fingers in and out of a fist. "The ones who took money?"

Alfie's typing slowed at the thoughtful tone that came from the larger man. Russell stood still as a statue again, but there was something tense and almost dangerous about him now that hadn't been there before. Alfie rubbed the knuckles of the hand resting on the keyboard, shifting in his seat. "I-I suppose, but it'd probably be a waste of time. You'd have to track down the author, and then circumvent all of tricks they're using to cover their tracks, and then compare it to where the malware itself was sending data, and so forth, and so forth. Usually it's not worth the effort. It's why people keep doing these things. They know they can get away with it."

Russell placed a hand on the back of his desk chair, and the other on the desk. He cornered Alfie between himself and the wall, looking the man in his wide green eyes. Russell closed the space so that it was only those two. The rest of the room did not exist in this bubble. Alfie's breath hitched, and Russell tightened his grip on the chair. "But you find them, yes? Is possible?"

Alfie sunk in his chair as the large man loomed over him, blocking the light from the room. He was suffocating. The chair beneath him creaked under the man's weight, and his computer hummed transferring files. Alfie wondered if it would hold. He gripped the seat of the chair, bracing his feet on the floor for the inevitable fall. "I suppose?"

"Good."

Russell slid away from Alfie like a puff of smoke. He sat on the bed, slapping his hands on his knees. Alfie lifted himself higher on the chair, having slunk down until his back was curved and his rear was on the edge of the seat. His hand trembled as he saved the file on his computer after the transfer finished.

Russell clamped a hand down on the man's shoulder as he leaned over again. "Now, find them."

Two hours, a removal script written and submitted to all the major Anti-Malware software authors, about fifty underground chats later, and Alfie was still searching for some hint at who created the blasted malware *FlowerMantis69*. The muscles in his fingers burned from the constant typing, joints stiff and unwieldily. If he knew he was going to be doing this much work, Alfie would have picked up his wrist braces on the way out the door. The constant tension from Russell staring at his every move hadn't helped the issue much, either.

The man wasn't human. Alfie had never met anyone who could sit that still, for so long watching. Staring. You couldn't even tell the man was breathing half the time with his smooth intake of air and silent exhales. If he didn't blink irregularly, Alfie would have just assumed he was a robot and called it a day. Well, and eating. The breathing statue needed nourishment as much as everyone else, the only hint that he was truly made of the same flesh and blood as the rest of humanity.

Russell the Human Golem had left to pick up some sort of dinner about twenty minutes ago, so Alfie took this brief opportunity to scream at Sam before he came back and Russell resumed his staring with the addition of Chinese take out.

"You could have mentioned your friend was insane when you asked me to help him!" Alfie shouted in his phone, while simultaneously arguing semantics with some hack-job programmer responsible for an automatic wiping program in the latest chat room. Alfie shifted the phone cradled between his ear and his shoulder. The flip-phone may not have been the latest touch screen, but Alfie was so deep in electronics all the time, he wanted at least one gadget that was simple. The way this job should have been. "Because really, knowing your friend was a lunatic seems like something I should have been briefed on before I got here, don't you think?"

"What? He didn't hurt you or anything, did he?" Sam asked on the other end. The man leaned back into his beanbag chair, as he tapped the ankle of the bikini dressed girl playing solitaire next to his feet. He bit his hand to keep from laughing as Alfie freaked out on the other line. Russell had that effect on people, it was true. Sam wouldn't have had it any other way. "You sound fine enough to me if you can complain this much."

"No, he hasn't hurt me, but that's not the point!" Alfie hissed.

Alfie tapped the keyboard loudly, each hit a determined force of aggression. Work through the pain! He'd argued the search for the programmers was pointless after the initial command, but Russell repeated his orders and pointed at the computer. Alfie would have continued his disagreement, but one more good look in those crazed blue eyes and muscles of steel larger than his head had Alfie agreeing to the man's bidding faster than a Yes Man.

This was Sam's fault.

Alfie stopped typing, to hold the phone more properly. He tapped the keys as the man on the other end started some idiotic discussion about remote hard drive reformatting. Alfie rubbed between his eyes. "He's got me hunting down the people who scammed him, and he keeps *staring*. He looks chilled as an icicle, but his eyes, man, they are on fire. Like he could burn something alive just by glaring at it. If looks could kill, I think he could do it."

Sam paused on the other end of the phone. The hilarity of the situation shattered like the legs of a cheater in a casino. Sam sat up straight in his chair, crossing his legs and bracing himself on his knees. "Hey, Al."

"Don't call me that," Alfie said. He said goodbye on a few chats and pulled up another window. Another dead end chatroom, and now Sam was teasing him. Alfie's day just couldn't any better than this! Alfie introduced himself on the chat, while Sam breathed on the other end of the line. "You know I hate that nickname."

"Right, about Russell," Sam said. He weighed the odds of whether or not dropping in on Russell's apartment right now would be better or worse for Al. When Russell got his mind set on something, there wasn't much you could do to stop him. It'd be like trying to stop a steam roller with a dandelion. "Just do what he tells you, okay? No matter what it is, just do it."

Alfie stopped typing mid-sentence. The curser blinked on and off right after the letter "o" in what would be the word "stop." Sam sounded serious. He never sounded serious. The man was a walking example of irresponsibility and playboy tendencies. Alfie's voice and grip on the phone tightened as he asked, "Why?"

"Look, he's pretty calm most of the time, in fact almost all the time, but that guy has a trigger temper." Sam rubbed his bottom lip with the back of his thumb. He hadn't been there to see it in person, but Alfie had described Russell's "Out for Blood" face pretty well. Definitely in his best interest to monitor, but not interfere directly. Sam hoped his computer contact would stay off the man's radar. Russell at work got messy, and Sam needed Alfie as his I.T. guy. "I wouldn't press it."

"You weren't joking about that hurting me thing earlier, were you?" Alfie asked. He rubbed his finger along the coarse grains of the chair seat, the chat room forgotten. He winced when he caught his finger on a splinter. The tiny piece of wood was an omen. Alfie stared at the blinking curser. "This guy could actually hurt me, couldn't he?"

Sam squirmed into his chair loud enough that the shifting beads under the fabric could be heard through the phone. "Not if you do what he says?"

The unsure question hung in the air like a fog of frozen breath. It chilled Alfie's bones, and sped up his heart rate. He bit his finger to force out the splinter. He tasted blood. "Sam, who is this guy?"

"My co-worker?"

"Sam!"

The door to the tiny apartment clicked open, bringing with it the smell of take-out Chinese in its salted glory. Grease from fried wontons soaked the bottom of the bag, the thin paper holding not quite enough to contain it. Russell closed the door behind him, shifting the bags in his grip.

A tiny smile appeared on Russell's face seeing Alfie still sitting at his small corner desk. He was on the phone, and his computer was open with text flying by on the tiny window. Hard at work. Russell's heart swelled in pride of finding someone to combat the laziness that dripped off his usual company of Sam. He also would not deny that it was nice coming home to find another warm body in his apartment. It felt less sterile and empty.

Russell tightened his grip on the top of the brown paper bag. For some reason, none of his co-workers liked to stay at his place. Not even his partner Sam hung around long after work or jobs. If they spent time out together at all, it was in the field or at Sam's plush apartment downtown.

"I'm home," Russell said. He didn't think Alfie heard him come in. The poor boy jumped as he turned around. The phone was clutched to his ear, an old flip model with a tiny screen and large button keys.

Russell liked that. Low-tech.

Alfie just kept surprising him.

"Hi," Alfie said, hand shaking as he held the phone next to his ear. He swallowed, forcing his active imagination down his throat with the knot. "Welcome back."

"He's home?," Sam asked. He clicked his tongue and decided to make a quick exit before Russell could grab the phone. "I need to go. Just remember, do whatever he says!"

Sam hung up the phone with a solid, deafening, *click*. Alfie whimpered, biting his lip hard to smother the sound before Russell noticed. Alfie pulled his phone down and stared at the End Call screen with the resolve of a man headed for the gallows.

While Russell was happy to have company for dinner, Alfie wondered just what the heck he'd gotten into.

Russell reached behind his desk and pulled out a short TV tray, unfolding it with a quick *snap*. He set it between himself and Alfie, wiping off the top with a clean napkin. Alfie typed furiously at his keyboard, shoulders hunched and doing everything possible to look nonchalant. Russell pretended he hadn't seen the young man throw his cell phone back into his bag as though it burnt him a second ago, or that he knew the cause of the young man's worry. He had a gut feeling Alfie had been talking with Sam, likely still upset and complaining about Russell's request. Or worried for his safety and wanted to know more about Russell. Alfie's caution stung, but did not come as a surprise.

Alfie was a tiny man who repaired computers. Of course Russell scared him.

Russell placed the tray of General Tso's chicken and white rice on the tabletop, and kept his his own meal of Lo Mein and fried rice to his lap. He set a fork next to the chicken, pushing both toward Alfie's side of the table. Russell pulled out a fork for himself, and ate holding his tray up near his chest. Alfie kept typing, stopping only for a moment to rub his nose.

Russell pushed the tray of chicken closer toward Alfie. "Eat."

Alfie reached over with one hand, still typing with the other, and used the fork to eat as commanded. His eyes never left the screen, forcing his body to lean awkwardly as he tried not to drop any food on the clean floors. Russell moved the small table closer to him, without any indication of whether he was annoyed or not. Alfie smiled at him in what was hopefully translated as a thank you, but kept going with his work. It was rude, but he wanted this job done as soon as possible. That and any break in the current conversation he was having would hurt his rhythm. In a world where no one trusted anyone on the other end of the screen, losing his concentration with certain people wasn't something Alfie could afford.

"Thanks," he said, around a mouthful of tangy rice and chicken when the conversation in the secure chat started to slow. He licked the corner of his mouth when a piece of rice got stuck between a tooth and his gums. Russell was watching him work, eating quietly. His shoulders were slumped, a far cry from his previous sitting at attention, and Alfie felt a bit bad by the way he'd been acting. Despite Sam's warnings, he really hadn't *done* anything all that bad, yet. Maybe Alfie should try a little harder to be nice. He pointed at the chicken, and said, "I swear, programmers live off this stuff."

"Would not know," Russell said. He ate, watching the smaller man alternate between eating chicken, licking sauce of his lip, and typing entire sentences faster than Russell could a single word. Every once in a while he'd break the pattern to shove his glasses up his nose, but for the most part he was like a well oiled machine; dedicated. Russell ate a bite of his noodles, happy yet again that they had something in common. "How long does this take?"

"Depends on how quick the folks on these forums figure out I'm faking." Alfie typed a furious response at some idiot claiming he invented the first piece of malware. "One of these guys will know who made the one who got your machine, but if they find out I'm a spy, I'm out of luck."

"Approximate?" Russell stirred his noodles with the fork.

Alfie shook his head, shoving his fork into an egg roll sitting on the side. He took a large bite out of the flakey crust and used his hand to catch bits of the stuffings before they could land on Russell's spotless floors. He licked a piece of chicken off his palm. "Wish I could tell you, but for both our sakes, let's hope it's quick."

"Quick" turned into a little over six hours of typing and pretending to be an anarchy enthusiast.

Alfie had gone through six usernames with unique personas, four fake IP routers, and two VPNs hunting down the programmer behind *FlowerMantis69*. His fingers typed on automatic as his eyes threatened to close on him like a loose garage door. Too tired to even be sore anymore, Alfie pressed on to the finish line. He'd cornered the creators responsible, or at least was pretty sure he had. Alfie recognized a typical typing pattern style signature in both the malware and their user info, but he had some egos to fan before they'd cough up a confession.

Alfie glanced at his client. Russell watched him, calm as a tree in the middle of the woods. Arms crossed, feet flat on the ground and back straight in a better mood than before. After cleaning up dinner, he'd taken that pose and kept it. He'd been sitting at perfect, military style attention for six hours. Alfie turned back to his monitor. Sweat beaded on his skin just thinking about the sort of patience and diligence required to do that. Sure Russell was proving to be nicer than he looked, but it was still intimidating.

Alfie sat up in his seat, looking at the next line in the chat.

> You don't think I created it huh, wise guy?

"I think I got him," Alfie said, typing a sarcastic response. It looked like anger was what he needed to get this guy to slip up. "As soon as he posts what I think he's going to, I'll know for sure."

"Good," Russell said. He stood up and leaned over Alfie on the chair, cornering him again with a hand on the chair back, and the other on the desktop. Russell tapped Alfie's shoulder with his index finger. "You did good."

"Come, on." Alfie leaned forward in his seat, urging the screen to blink up the line of text he so desperately wanted to see. One line and he could go home. *One line.* "Come on!"

A block of text popped up: a unique key that only the creator would have bothered to know buried in the deepest pit of the original code.

"That's him, no question." Alfie fell back in his seat, brushing against Russell's arm and flinched. When had Russell moved? Alfie steadied himself, even as he became aware of Russell's arms trapping him in the seat. *Nothing to be scared of. Russell wanted to see the screen. That's all.* Alfie pointed at the appropriate username. "That guy is responsible for your wiped data and stolen money. Want to yell at him? Fair warning, though, he'll probably log off as soon as you do."

Russell squeezed the back of the chair, the wood creaking under his hold. "Where is he?"

"In the chatroom?" Alfie asked, hesitantly. He'd found the guy. What more did Russell want? Alfie pointed at the name again, just in case he got confused with Alfie's screen name. "He's that guy right there. If you want to tell him off in person for ripping you off, this is your chance."

The blond man grit his teeth, sucking in a breath through them. Alfie didn't understand him. He wasn't in the business. Russell moved his hand to squeeze Alfie's shoulder. He could feel the thin man's bone right through the skin with barely a touch. Alfie needed more meat on him, but that was not important right now. Russell hissed, "No. The man on the other end of the screen. *Where* is he?"

Alfie winced under the man's heavy grip, tempted to shove the hand off. He felt the bruise forming under Russell's massive hand with every twitch of the tense grip. Alfie asked, "His physical location?"

"Yes! I want to know where man is." Russell grinned wolfishly, flexing his fingers on Alfie's bony shoulder. He was getting it! "You tell me."

"I don't know." Alfie could feel his bones shifting against each other in his shoulder. "I'd have to track that down."

"Do this," Russell said. He moved to put his hands on both shoulders. His thumbs rested on Alfie's collarbone, and his fingers touching the man's neck. Russell nodded firmly to confirm his confidence in Alfie's abilities. "I know you can."

"Right," Alfie said. Russell's tone left no room for argument. Unsure about how right Sam was about Russell's patience with the larger man's hands around his neck, Alfie shifted until the massive man went back to holding him down with one hand. His fingers danced among the keys opening windows and his personal software. The malware's programmer true location was as hidden as Alfie's own, but it'd take time to crack the actual location. Time Alfie wasn't sure he had.

Or then again, maybe their guilty party wasn't as prepared as Alfie thought he was. Only thirty minutes of ego-padding and tracking behind the user's back later, and *FlowerMantis69's* true IP address was logged and backed up on Alfie's laptop.

"Got it," he breathed out. Alfie shoved his fingers in his eyes and pulled his hands down, nearly sobbing in relief. "I know where he is."

"Good." Russell laughed, shaking the man's shoulder. He liked this Alfie. He was a good man. Worked hard. Followed instructions well. Knew his craft. Who knew Sam could keep such good company? Russell shook Alfie's shoulder lightly and pointed at the screen. "The man is still there, in this 'chat,' yes?"

"Yeah?" Alfie looked up, seeing that crazed look again; Russell's blue eyes were on fire.

Russell grinned, "I want to tell him something."

CHAPTER 3

"WHY ARE YOU giggling, Kirk?" Ross asked. He leaned over the back of his cohort's chair, stuffing half of a bread roll in his mouth. The crumbs spilled on Kirk's shoulder, leaving a mess of his pressed suit jacket. Ross didn't bother to brush them off, and instead took another bite. "Are you sexting again?"

"Nah, it's this guy in the chat, man. He's gushing over our *Mantis* and what it did to his computer." Kirk threw back another response on his keyboard.

Kirk shoved Ross back a foot to get away from his poppy-seed reeking breath. He wiped his shoulder off, spilling the crumbs onto the wood floor. Kirk scowled at the mess, rolling his eyes. They needed to get a bigger place. The small cottage they were using had two rooms downstairs with one full of kitchen stuff, and the other packed to capacity with computers and servers. Living on top of each other, Kirk felt like a sardine in a can. He could do without Ross' crumbs on himself or his equipment.

"He thinks I'm like a god of programming." Kirk entered the next line of text informing the lovely stranger he could free to continue. At least Kirk had entertainment in the cramped living conditions. There was only so much you could do stuck inside all day. Kirk petted the side of his mouse with his thumb in small circles. "It's downright hilarious what an idiot this guy is."

Ross licked a crumb out of the corner of his teeth, and finished the last of his poppy-seed roll. "Looks like he hasn't replied in a bit."

Kirk dropped his hands behind his head, and crossed his ankles under the desk. Was there anything better than having your work appreciated?

Even if it was from a lowly, gushing sycophant? He brushed his hair back with his hand, digging his fingers into his scalp in a personal massage. Kirk could chat with this guy all night. A "Maestro of Code" indeed. "Yeah, must be thinking of the perfect thing to say about my awesome."

Ross sat in his chair behind Kirk, and pulled up the next victim of their Mantis. The malware protection community had already gotten their source code and provided ways to quarantine and clean it out somehow to the general public. It was putting a serious dent in their profits, and Ross could only be thankful for folks who didn't update their protection software. Only a fellow hacker could have figured it out that quick and turned around a fix in less than two days. There was nothing worse than a traitor who turned in their peers. "Just concentrate on our latest project instead of bragging in chatrooms. That thing'll make papers, just you wait."

"Don't you know it," Kirk said, turning his attention to the second screen on his desk. He was halfway through a line of code when a chime sounded on the first monitor. "Oh, he posted another message."

    Hello.

Kirk didn't move, watching the screen oddly with his narrow nose scrunched. Ross rolled over to look over his shoulder again. He glanced up at the earlier conversation, and this sudden break was unusual. Ross asked, "This someone new?"

"I don't know. The username's the same and it's supposed to be a private chat." Kirk dropped his chin on his knuckles. *What was going on over there?* "Oh, he's typing. There's the next part…"

    You took my money. I find you.

"It's a bluff," Kirk said. He ignored the chat and rolled back over to their *QueenMantis*. He scrunched his shoulders. So it wasn't a fan, after all. It was a victim. All that praise and heartfelt appreciation was a ruse for confirmation. Kirk hunched his shoulders, his fingers hit the keys like lead weights, heavy and thudding. What a mood killer. "No one's going to find us, and even if they do, that guy's back home in the States and we're here. What's he going to do?"

"Yeah, nothing to worry about," Ross said, rubbing the tips of his

Man On The Other End

fingers together. His body was on edge. Something about those last two messages setting the hairs on his arms straight. Ross heard another chime. "What's that next line?"

Kirk froze in his chair reading the text:

I break you.

25

CHAPTER 4

ALFIE WHISTLED AT the computer screen as he shut down all of the chats, re-set all of his cloaking modes, and leaned back in his seat. Russell was a man of few words, but he didn't seem to need many. Alfie crossed his arms on the desk as his screen-saver activated and licked side of his mouth. "That'll spook 'um."

"Only fair give warning." Russell slapped Alfie's shoulder, before heading to the back closet. He pulled out a duffle from the floor and placed it on his bed. Russell opened the bag, and scooted the medical kit and pre-prepared overnight supplies to the far corner to make room for more. He'd have to get a new cell phone at the main office, and then make flight reservations as soon as he got his destination. Russell opened his trunk and considered which clothes he was going to bring as he asked, "Where is he?"

"Little town in Lithuania," Alfie said. He dropped an arm over the back of the chair as he watched the larger man pull clothes from his chest and re-fold them smaller as he stuffed them into his bag. Alfie rubbed his shoulder where the man's hand had claimed its home for the past half-hour, wincing at the sore shock that shot through his arm. He was checking for a bruise the second he got home. "What are you doing?"

"Packing," Russell said. He dumped a neatly folded stack of clothes on the edge of his bed as he continued to search through the trunk. Russell placed a pair of spare shoes on the top of the stack. "You and I are going."

"To Lithuania?" Alfie said, scrunching his mouth into a question. He mouthed what Russell said to himself, eyebrows digging closer together as he processed the words.

Alfie leapt from the chair.

The programmer pointed an accusing finger at the larger man. "And what do you mean 'You and I?' "

"Do not worry. I pay." Russell transferred a pair of pants and an extra shirt to the duffle bag. Two pairs of socks, fresh underwear, and a small travel bag of toiletries already packed for emergencies from under his sink followed. The younger man stood next to his computer, eyes wide and tense. Russell slapped Alfie on the back. "We leave tonight. You have name of town, yes?"

"Yes," Alfie said, wheezing to get his breath back from the hit. "But no, I'm not going anywhere. Certainly not to Lithuania—What is that and why are you putting it in the bag!"

"Police baton." Russell held up the folded weapon and whipped it in the air, extending it to its full length. He spun it once, showing off it's lean, sturdy shape. Alfie stared at the weapon like he'd never seen one before, and considering the young man's disposition, that was likely true. Russell flipped it over and smashed it back into the folded position on the top of his trunk. "It is my favorite."

"Favorite for what?" Alfie felt his breath pick up, on the verge of hyperventilating. Sam said he had a trigger temper. That meant punching and hitting things in a sudden rage. He was packing weapons. That implied premeditation. *What is going on?* Alfie stepped back, placing the wooden chair between him and Russell. "What would you need those for?"

Russell threw two gun cases and a rolled pack of knives into the bag. Torture was fun, but it was always nice to have a quick finish when you got to the end. Unlike some of his co-workers, he found the sobbing and whining that followed the breaking of limbs to be annoying. It grated on his ears and wasted time. "I am going to make them pay. Break legs, rip out fingernails, cut iris out of eye, that sort of thing. You know, torture."

"For stealing thirty grand?" Alfie not-so-subtly closed his laptop and shoved it in his messenger bag, the cords still dangling from where they were attached to Russell's computer. This man was crazy. The second Russell turned his back to shift things around in his bag, Alfie ripped the cords free and shoved them into the bag while he strapped it onto his person. He slowly sidestepped toward the front door, one hand still on the chair in case he needed to throw it at the giant. The second he hit the hallway, Alfie was going to run. As fast as his barely-in-shape legs would carry him. "Doesn't that strike you as a bit extreme?"

"No. They took my money." Russell zipped the bag up and threw it over his shoulder. He saw Alfie had already done the same, clutching the bag and its computer inside to his chest. *Good.* It was nice to know he was in as big of a hurry. "They shall pay me back double."

Alfie's eyes watered when Russell moved to stand between him and the door. *So much for running.* "But what do you need *me* for?"

"To confirm we have right people." Russell tapped the strap of his pack on his shoulder. He hiked the bag higher up, happy to have its comfortable weight on his back. "With what I plan to do, it is very important I have guilty party. No room for mistake."

"You want me to check his computer or something when we get there?" Alfie asked, unsure if that's what he wanted. "That it?"

"Yes!" Russell said, smiling. He really liked this one. Russell had never met a civilian this wonderful before. Let alone someone Sam knew who wasn't a hooker or a louse on society. Russell pulled an arm around Alfie's shoulder and pulled him into a side hug. "And then I shall beat them until they beg their mothers to save them."

Alfie flinched in Russell's embrace.

Russell rubbed the smaller man's shoulder. *Ah, weak constitution.* Russell made a mental note to not go into further detail of his work. It wouldn't do to scare Alfie away so soon. Keepers were essential for a proper job, and Sam wasn't here. "Do not worry, my friend. I shall not make you watch."

Alfie was in the room with a madman, and it was all Sam's fault. His knees buckled.

"Come!" Russell said, gripping the man's shoulder tighter so he would not fall over. "We stop at your place. I call for ride, and you pack bag. Yes?"

Russell loomed over him, tall and unmoving as a monolith. Alfie was sure his voice cracked like an acne-ridden teenager when he repeated back, "Yes!"

"Your friend is *crazy!* You told me to do what he tells me, but this is too much!" Alfie hissed into the phone trapped between his shoulder and his ear as he threw a few pairs of clothes in a bag. Russell, in the meantime, looked through a circuit-board photography book from Alfie's cluttered coffee table in the living room. Pretending to be harmless, but Alfie was onto his game! Russell was still only one room away, though, and Alfie in no way wanted that man to hear him. "He wants me to go with him to *Lithuania* to hunt down a pair of rogue programmers that ripped him off!"

"That sounds like, Russell." Sam hummed, flipping through a girly magazine on the other end of the line. Alfie sounded freaked, but Sam knew his partner Russell well enough to know there was no getting out of it now. Guy was stubborn. Sam wondered if he'd have to find a new tech-expert after all, or if Russell would look out for little Alfie. It could really go either way, especially after Sam received the text from his partner that Alfie was playing Keeper for the week. Poor kid probably didn't even realize he'd earned the temporary title. Sam tilted the magazine to the side to get a better look at a girl in the polka-dot bikini. "He broke a pick-pocket's fingers once when they snatched his wallet. Smashed them so hard together one of the bones popped out of the socket and through the skin."

Alfie took the phone down and stared at the screen. Sam had said that distractedly. Like that was normal behavior for his friend. What had happened to his serious-mode earlier warning him about Russell's temper? Alfie could even hear the tell-tale signs of magazine pages flipping on the other end of the phone. *Of course.* Alfie stuffed shirts in a bag. "Excuse me?"

"Russell doesn't like thieves. He grew up with them and they left a bad impression." Sam licked his finger to flip another page. "They disgust him. He hates them. However you want to put it."

Alfie covered his mouth as he hissed into the phone. "He's going to *kill* these people."

"Yup," Sam answered. If he'd know this would be such a pain, Sam wouldn't have bothered helping Russell out. Really, you do a guy a favor to bring him up to speed with the internet and this is how he repays you! Typical. Alfie, too. Sam got him much needed income, and he's complaining about something as insignificant as a hit job. They should both be much more appreciative of Sam's hard work. He flipped to the next page; black & white striped one-piece. "And slowly, no doubt."

"He wants me to go with him!" Alfie slapped a hand over his mouth, darting his eyes at the door. There was no sound from the other room. He whispered, "Did you hear that part? He's got me packing for the trip!"

"And you should do what he tells you."

"But—"

"Look," Sam said, cutting Alfie off. "He's happy with you right now, right?"

"Yes, but what does that—"

"Then make sure he stays that way, or the guy at the end of his automatic is going to be *you*, and not some loser kids in Lithuania." Sam shifted on the other end of the line. He closed his magazine and rubbed the space between his eyes with his thumb in a steady circular motion. Alfie needed to calm down or this was going to be much worse than it had to be. Sam tried to keep his voice soothing for his techno-rabbit. "But seriously, Alfie. The guy's a professional. Do what he says, and you'll be fine. Trust me. I've been his partner for a long time, and he only murders targets and people who piss him off. Otherwise he's harmless."

Alfie's hands shook as he gathered his toothbrush and toothpaste from the sink. He shoved them one by one into the ziplock bag. *I'm going to die. I'm going to die. I'm going to die.* "Good to know."

"Really, there's nothing to worry about," Sam said. "If he likes you, you're fine. Keep him happy, and you'll have a great time. He'll pay for everything, he'll get the job done, and you'll get a free European sight-seeing trip out of the deal."

"But what if I screw up?" Alfie whispered into the phone line, throwing his toiletries into his duffle. He shoved them in the side pocket, separate from his clothes and shoes. Socks followed, with a few spare USB cords thrown in for good measure. "Then what?"

"Are you going to steal from him?"

"No."

"Then you're golden. Have fun in Lithuania, and bring me back some cookbooks. I love their food."

"Yeah, I'll try and think about that while I try and not *die!*" Alfie zipped his bag up with a jerk of his arm. "And we get back, you tell me what you really do for a living, Mr. I'm-in-the-Secret-Service!"

"Deal." Sam laughed over the phone, having forgotten what he told Alfie to explain why he never talked about work. If he'd known it'd come out sooner or later, he probably wouldn't have bothered with the lie. Sam smirked into his hand. "And who knows, maybe I can get you in if you like it?"

"No!" Alfie growled, hanging up on Sam before he could say anything else. He was going to get Sam for this if it was the last thing he did.

"Lot of help you are," Alfie said to the blank home screen.

Alfie tossed his duffle over his shoulder, snatching his carrier bag containing his trusty laptop off the floor with the other hand. He trudged out into the the main floor or his apartment after kicking his door closed, but Russell was no where to be seen. The art book was left open on his couch, and Alife could see the wires Russell had shifted to sit scrunched in the corner, but there was no sign of the giant man.

Maybe he'd gotten tired of waiting and had left already? Alfie though, shifting the heavy bags on his arm. He pulled it up higher on his shoulder when the bag slipped down. Between his clothes, laptop, and technical gear the pack weighed down his shoulder almost more than Alfie could handle. He rubbed at the spot near the strap, hoping he could carry this stuff for as long as it would take to escape.

Alfie may have screamed when his duffle and carrier bags were plucked from his shoulder, but you would be hard pressed to get him to admit it later. The bags disappeared over Russell's back as he threw them over one shoulder in a single movement. He stood next to Alfie, the hallway bathroom door open behind him. Alfie rubbed his shoulder, the flesh red and already relieved at the lack of weight. "There you are."

"Yes," Russell said, lifting the straps to indicate the bags. "I carry."

"O-okay," Alfie said, walking like a rigid wooden door behind him. Russell picked up his own bags, transferring them to his other shoulder. He held it all with one hand like the mammoth he was with the same ease as if he were carrying a bag of air. Russell walked across Alfie's apartment like he owned it, not a care in the world on his stone-like face. Alfie followed when the man opened the door and waited for him to grab his keys.

Alfie locked the door, twisting the knob to be sure as they stood in the hallway. Whether it was to double-check against thieves or kill time, Alfie wasn't sure yet. Russell slapped a hand on Alfie's shoulder again, but from the back this time. He leaned over him, cornering him between the man's muscled form and the door. Alfie's chest tightened, and body refused to move, suffocating from Russell's body heat. Alfie felt the man breathing in his ear, and a wave of nausea sent shivers to every inch of his body.

"Do not worry so," Russell whispered gently. He rubbed the man's shoulder with his thumb, like he was petting a small kitten on the head. "I like you. Sam is right, you are safe with me."

Alfie's throat was thick with his own tongue, so he could only nod until Russell released his shoulder with a gentle pat following. He stood stock still, staring at the number 4-45A on his apartment door. When his feet came back around from their temporary strike, he followed Russell out of the building.

He hoped Sam and Russell were right.

Alfie looked both ways, his arms crossed and sliding from foot to foot as they stood on the main street outside his apartment building. The wind ruffled his loose hair, and he could smell the grilled onions from the hot dog cart on the corner. Alfie waved at his neighbors as they slowed down to see him standing next to the Adonis-like man that was Russell. Not exactly Alfie's usual company; usually he was just plain alone. Russell stood at attention, body rigid as he held the bags and kept his eyes looking forward. Alfie scuffed his foot along a crack in the sidewalk. Russell probably got these sort of looks with or without Alfie standing next to him.

After about twenty minutes, Alfie watched a man pull up to the roadway in a dark-blue sedan with black tinted windows. He looked like he was straight out of a mob movie, and Alfie rubbed the top of his arms. Russell walked to the window as it rolled down and held his hand out. A man in a grey suit and designer sunglasses snorted and handed Russell a phone, slapping it into the larger man's palm like he'd done this too many times before. Alfie watched the exchange from the corner of his eye, pointedly keeping his direct attention on a decorative shrub. Russell returned to his side as the man drove away.

Alfie looked at the little black phone, and held in the laugh. Russell stared at the little device like it was the devil. Alfie covered his mouth with his hand. "I see you upgraded to a touch-screen."

"All they had," Russell said. He stared at the thing for two minutes, before he unlocked the screen with a rough swipe of his finger. The "contacts" button was large and dead center on the miniature screen, a blessing. Russell tapped on it, and searched the list for the main office number. He borrowed Alfie's phone earlier before the smaller man began packing, and if what they said was true, a back up of his contacts should already be on the phone. Russell reminded himself to thank Sam for setting that up. "It should work."

"You got that quick, too." Alfie said, thinking of how shifty that whole exchange had looked. Speaking of, Alfie looked at the plain black duffle hanging next to his own. He felt like the bag was transparent, even though the contents were hidden behind the thick meshing. Alfie glanced one way down the street, and then the other. No one was out, and they were alone for the moment. The taxi they called from the front desk would be there any second, and Alfie just had to ask. Lowering his voice, he said, "How are you going to get all those weapons on the plane?"

"Private airline," Russell said. He had been counting down the seconds for when the constant ball of twitching, fidgeting Alfie would say something concerning the illegality of this trip's nature. The questioning was predicted. Nervous people couldn't help themselves, and the words always came spilling out eventually. Though, with Alfie, it was not as annoying as Russell assumed it would be. "We will not even be walking through the main terminal."

"You got us a private flight all the way to Lithuania in less than two hours?" Alfie asked, not caring that his voice rose above a whisper. He'd figured out Sam and this guy were part of an unlawful organization after all the secrecy and plots to kill people, but he didn't realize just how high up they were. What sort of mafia was he dealing with that they could afford a jet across the ocean at the drop of a hat? "That's sort of incredible."

"Boss owed favor," Russell said. He shifted his grip on the bags, and placed his new phone in his front pants pocket. "Reward for past job I had yet to collect."

"Nice boss," Alfie said, more to himself than anything.

"No. Cruel man. No mercy, no tolerance, and very short-tempered." Russell placed a hand on Alfie's head, and ruffled the brown hair through his fingers. Russell couldn't help himself. Such a short and adorable man was asking for it. Russell patted the top of Alfie's head. "He owe me favor, nothing more."

Russell paused, and rubbed his thumb on Alfie's head. "I hope you never meet him."

You and me both, Alfie thought, letting out a breath when Russell removed his hand. Alfie rubbed his arm through his long-sleeved button shirt. He dressed up a bit for the trip, but forgo the tie. Russell donned a turtleneck for the occasion, a steal-grey, and wore his same bluejeans from yesterday. Alfie was probably over dressed, but better to be over than under when heading off to kill people, right?

Their taxi arrived a few minutes after, and Alfie dumped himself into a seat. Not two hours ago, Alfie was hounding down a couple cyber criminals. Now he was in a car with a professional criminal out for their blood. Alfie slunk in his seat, clutching his computer bag to his chest. He refused to let his safety blanket be thrown in the trunk.

Russell read a paperback while Alfie sulked, sinking into a dull pit of boredom. The cityscape was a mass of grey beyond the window, dotted with the colors of people's clothing. Alfie shifted in the stained taxi seat, listening to Russell flip pages. Said boredom quickly won out over his petulance. Alfie turned in his seat, so that he was half-facing the larger man. "What are you reading?"

"Thriller." Russell turned to the next page. The novel's cracked spine barely held together the torn, yellowed pages. It had survived many a boring traveling trip; his favorite on-the-job read. "The serial killer is amateurish, but I like the detective."

Is that irony? Alfie wondered, but let it be. He scuffed his foot on the floorboard. "Never got into thrillers, myself. Sci-fi was always more interesting."

"Those go over head. Too many computers and automation." Russell closed his book at the end of the chapter, and set it in his lap. The world passed by them in the window. He saw trees and people. Civilians going about their lives in the daylight, without a care or worry. All of them inconsequential. However, the once civilian next to him no longer fit in the same lump of people: He was Alfie. It was rude to read while talking with someone with a name, wasn't it? Russell turned to face Alfie as he continued, "Prefer more manual things."

"Big guy like you?" Alfie asked, shoving his glasses up his face with a crooked grin. He straightened back up, thumping his back on the seat. "I don't see it."

"I am very good with my hands." Russell lifted an eyebrow, picking up on the joke. Alfie was relaxed enough to banter. *Good.* As such, Alfie surely wouldn't mind if Russell made use of his things until they got onto the plane. He tucked his book away in Alfie's bag as the taxi pulled up to the airport. The man protested at the invasion with a glare and a brief question of motives, but it was as effective as a kitten hissing. "We are here."

Alfie scooted out of the car, while Russell paid the driver with a hundred. The little ticket window had said forty. *Quite the tip*, Alfie thought to himself. Russell picked up their bags from the back of the trunk, leaving Alfie to wait for him on the sidewalk.

When the cab drove off, Alfie asked, "Where'd you get the money for this anyway? Didn't your bank say you were cleaned out? I know it takes longer than a day to process insurance and money replacement after a theft."

"I made withdrawal from joint account with Sam," Russell said, hoisting the bags over his shoulder. The back gates lead to the tarmac and private hangers, and he headed in that direction knowing well that Alfie would follow. He fished an ID out of his back pocket and flashed it at the guards standing at the entrance. They opened the section with no trouble and allowed the two to pass. "He said I could have as much as I want."

"And he begs me for discounts, the cheapskate." Alfie trailed along the walkway behind Russell, messenger bag hanging off his shoulder. The bag tapped against his side with a familiar weight while the chain-link fence passed them by. They turned down a sidewalk along the fence of the airfield, heading toward a few hangers he could see clumped in the back, far away from the main terminal. Alfie shoved his hands in his pockets, shivering against the wind. "I'm charging him double the next time he wants me to fix his stupid server."

"That you should, my friend." Russell's mouth quirked into a tiny smile. "That you should."

Alfie climbed the movable stairs up to the small side door, wind blowing through his hair and ringing in his ears. The plane was smaller than he was expecting for a transatlantic flight, but it was still a decent size. Russell said they'd be stopping for fuel in Germany, but after that it was a straight shot to Lithuania. The steps shifted and whined under Alfie's weight, his hand strangling the rail as the metal rattled. This was the first time he'd ever gotten onto a plane that wasn't pulled up alongside the main airport terminal. Russell insisted Alfie went up the ladder first, and Alfie had a feeling it was to keep the timid programmer from sprinting last minute. Alfie took a step into the main area of the plane, standing straight and relaxing upon seeing the main cabin.

The center of the plane was open, save for a few center tables bolted into the floor. There were cup holders indented into the table on each end, and the carpet under the table was bright red. Eight sets of double chairs facing each other lined either side of the cabin, the seats wide and plush. Each one had a thin half table bolted into the wall between them, complete with their own built in cup-holders.

Alfie dropped his computer bag in the nearest chair, and dumped his duffle on the floor. He gaped at the crystal glasses that sat waiting in each perfectly sized notch on the small half tables. The goblets were already full of sparkling water with a cherry sitting in the center of the ice. Alfie was terrified to touch it.

Russell slid up behind him and put his things behind the chair opposite Alfie's choice. As an afterthought, he reached over for Alfie's bag and did the same for it. He slipped his paperback out of the computer bag while the young man stared at every little extravagant detail the boss decided necessary for his personal travel. Russell stretched his arms behind his head, mentally preparing himself for the long flight. He sat opposite Alfie when the programmer took his seat. Alfie gripped the armrests like he couldn't believe the leather lining them was real, before going back to inspecting the glasses in front of him. Russell opened his book, leaving the other man to explore at his leisure before take off.

Alfie gathered his courage, and picked up a crystal goblet. He lifted his glasses up to inspect the mark etched into the bottom. This thing was vintage, hand-cut crystal. A sleek gold rim shined up at him as clean and perfect as the stemware. Alfie dealt with expensive computer equipment all the time—machines totaling in the thousands with ram and parts—but this one cup alone had to cost about two to three hundred dollars. Alfie bought his flatware from the bargain bin at the local department store where he could get eight glass stems for fifteen bucks.

"You could keep that, if you like it so much," Russell said over his book. "Boss replaces dishes on the flight whenever mood strikes. Never seen same set twice."

Alfie flinched and set the glass down quickly, the liquid sloshing over the edge onto the table. He gasped and checked to make sure he didn't chip anything before using both hands to steady the glass by the flat base. Once he was sure it wasn't moving, he wiped up the bit of water with the edge of his sleeve. "It's pretty, but I don't think it would fit in with my decor."

"I don't know. Might spruce place up. Add class." Russell flipped a page. "If worried, I could ask permission?"

"No, that's fine! The less your boss knows about me, the better." Alfie slumped down in his seat, glancing out the oval window at the black runway. The sun beat down and shined off the planes in the distance making their ways down the open area. Russell's plane sat quietly, the engines humming softly as they sat in place. Their turn wasn't for another twenty minutes, so he had time to kill. Maybe Alfie could catch a nap before the take off.

Just as his eyes started to close, he caught sight of two figures out the window. Alfie sat up and watched as a man in a dark suit and a woman following approached the mobile stairs. "Hey, Russell."

"Yes?"

"Who are those guys getting on the plane?" Alfie asked as the two nearly completed their trip up the stairs.

A head covered in styled black hair dipped forward through the doorway, eyes hidden by dark shades. The rest of the body followed, revealing a slim figure in a tailored black suit that hugged every line like water. A white silk tie complimented the deep red button up-shirt, fancy enough enough for Alfie to wish he'd worn a tie, too. That man's suit had to cost more than his entire wardrobe put together. A girl followed him with blonde hair, and bright blue eyes. She wore a matching skirt-suit, minus the tie, and had a cat-shaped broach with emerald eyes tacked to her lapel. The man pulled off his sunglasses to reveal warm chocolate eyes that practically drowned in charisma. They froze Alfie in place.

The man chuckled, white teeth sparkling as neatly as the crystal. "Russ! Who's your scruffy new friend?"

Russell swiftly found his feet, and placed himself between the two invaders and his new Keeper. Alfie was not ready for this, and Russell couldn't control that man if he wanted to. His promise to keep Alfie alive would be void fairly quickly if things got out of control in the next few moments, or if that man thought Alfie was up for grabs. Many of his peers had lost a Keeper to those two due to negligence, or a simple turned eye. Russell would not be one of them. "Armand. Duchess. What are you doing here?"

"Boss likes to save money, what can I say?" Armand said, slipping his glasses into his thousand-dollar coat front pocket. He snapped his fingers and Duchess dragged their luggage into the main cabin, prompt and prim as her skirt-suit. She set both floral-print designer suitcases on the floor and folded her hands behind her back like a good girl. Armand clapped Russell on the shoulder, but kept his eyes on the brown-haired stranger with glasses. "We had a job scheduled in Munich next week, and since you guys were taking a plane out that way already, he bumped us up. We're pinching pennies! Isn't that wonderful?"

"So we drop you off?" Russell asked, moving just enough to block Armand's view of Alfie. He looked at the programmer like he was a piece of prime cut beef. It was rude. "Then you leave?"

"Not so much," Armand said, rubbing the edge of his chin. Russell's back was straighter than usual, and he was making an extra effort to play Mr. Shield. Looked like the man with scraggly hair had something to him more than a cute little snack. Armand thought, *Maybe he got a new partner.*

"Since we don't really know how long it'll actually take to chase down the bastards who took your money, you guys get to tag along while we do our job first," Armand gestured to himself and Duchess, "and then we get to tag along on your little trip and make sure you don't get too carried away. Sound good?"

Russell dropped his shoulders, and watched Armand saunter around him to look Alfie over. He knew he should have suspected how easily their leader gave up a plane, favor or not. "Boss say this?"

"Yup!" Armand could hear the resignation in Russ' voice. He was on board, no matter how reluctantly. Russ was loyal like that, or at least smart enough to know better than to argue. Armand smoothed down his eyebrows with his thumb. "It'll be a pleasure working with you again."

Russell clenched his fists, but took a few steps back to settle back down in his chair. They were both professionals. Russell and Armand could stay out of each others ways if they must. It wasn't like Sam was there to cause trouble, either. He had a feeling that unlike his usual Keeper, Alfie wouldn't be going out of his way to antagonize the Frenchmen. Russell closed his eyes, and listened to Duchess' heels walk across the carpet to settle into a chair at the other end of the plane. Maybe this trip would not be so bad.

Armand dropped into the seat beside Russell, and crossed his legs with ease under the half table. Russell glared, and Armand grinned right back at him. He tilted his head at the brunette across the table. "You never did say who your new little friend is. That's rude you know, Ruskie."

"I am not Russian," Russell said. His hands clenched the arm rests, the leather under his hands stretched thing.

"I know," Armand said. He shrugged off his coat and draped it over his arm, before straightening the black vest underneath. He lifted the crystal glass from the table and took a sip of the sparking water. Armand winked at Russell's little friend, and dumped the glass back, popping the cherry into his mouth. He plucked the stem out, tied into a knot of course, while tipping the glass full of ice at the nervous man occupying the seat across from him. "Is your friend a guest, replacing Sam as your new Keeper—since I don't see his obnoxious face anywhere—a fashion victim in need of my tender mercies, your new pet, or what? Give me a line here, Russ."

"This is Alfie Knight," Russell said, resolving not to scoot away from the Frenchman and the smell of his expensive cologne. "He is technical support, and not replacing Sam."

"Nice to meet you, Alfie Knight," Armand said, holding his hand out for a shake. The other man slowly put out his hand, the entire arm trembling in fright. Armand reached out and grabbed it when the boy froze about an inch from meeting. He gripped it tightly, amused at the fluttering pulse under the young mans skin. Armand loved how delightfully terrified he was. Russell really had found a good one here, hadn't he? This was going to be *fun*. "I'm Armand Dubois, hit man at your service."

Alfie's hand shook violently in the other man's iron grip. He felt like he was going to pass out any second. Sam was a dead man. Alfie swallowed, and pretended his voice didn't crack. "Pleasure."

"Oh," Armand added as an afterthought while still holding the man's hand, "the lady back there is Duchess, and only Duchess. My personal assistant through thick and thin."

Alfie nodded, pulling his hand free from the other man's hold. He sunk as far into his seat as the fabric would allow, trying to bury himself from view. Armand sucked on a piece of ice, staring at Alfie over the drink with this predatory grin showing off perfect teeth like a tiger ready to spring. The main hatch closed, the engine started, and Alfie felt like crying.

"So this loser thinks that skipping town on us with two hundred grand and running off to Munich of all places is okay," Armand said. He took a deep drink from his glass to wet his throat, and finish off the last of the refreshing liquid. He unhooked the cuffs of his shirt sleeves, and rolled them back a few inches. "Really thought we wouldn't take offense at that. Can you believe it?"

"Yes," Russell said, longing for his book or sleep. Both of which were impossible at the moment. Six hours into the flight, and Armand had not stopped talking once the entire time. An endless stream of useless words that flooded the cockpit with inanity. He started the conversation off with news at the home front, and worked his way down to his suit ("The latest fashion out of Italy," Armand stressed.) and worked his way back around to the job he was assigned in Germany. No one could sleep through that.

Besides, if he fell asleep, Alfie would be left unguarded. With Armand. Russell rubbed the side of his eye and pretended his vengeance trip hadn't turned into a nightmare. "People do stupid things all time."

"True, true." Armand tapped his glass with a fork, awaiting the steward to refill his glass. He'd swapped out water for Vodka about an hour ago, and still felt it was a good decision. After the steward poured him a new cup, this time around leaving the bottle. Armand switched conversation venues for a more playful target.

"So, *Alfie*," Armand drew out the name like a fine wine should be poured, "what is it you do again?"

"Computer I.T.," Alfie said, trying to concentrate on his plate of food. Lamb chop, mashed potatoes, and green beans in gravy. To think he'd been impressed with the flatware. Four star restaurants didn't put out food this well prepared or tasty. Where on earth was the plane hiding the kitchen? Alfie couldn't have picked a better last meal himself. He speared a green bean with his fork and shoved it into the gravy. "I program on the side, too, I guess."

"And how did you meet dear little Ruskie?" Armand asked pleasantly, ignoring Russ' mumble of "Not a Russian."

"Sam." Short, quick, honest answers. Alfie wondered if that was the only way he'd get through the trip. Russell had been on edge, Alfie still shocked he could even tell that, from the moment Armand arrived on the plane. Alfie really didn't need much more incentive than that to set his own nerves and warning signs up to eleven. At least his blonde companion kept her distance on the other end of the plane. She reminded Alfie of a Stepford Wife, and he couldn't tell who was more disturbing. "I set up his personal server for him, and maintain it."

"So you're the one who helped him set up that wretched website he won't stop bothering the rest of us with. I like porn as much as the next guy, but everything on there is just so tacky it offends me," Armand said. He smirked around his glass when the programmer flinched. Armand tapped his finger on the tabletop. *So green.* "Half of me wants to strangle you now."

"Wouldn't you want to strangle Sam, instead?" Alfie offered, regretting it the second the words left his mouth. What if the guy didn't pick up on his joke? Who knew what these people took literally? He wanted revenge on Sam, but strangulation wasn't on the list. Crashing his site for a week seemed more appropriate. Alfie dropped his fork and held up his hands in a defensive shrug. "I'm just the hired help. Don't shoot the messenger and all that?"

"But those are the best ones to shoot," Armand said, leaning on his elbow. He sipped the last of his second cup, licking the last bits of it off his lips. "They always see it coming."

"Knock it off," Russell said. He grabbed Armand's glass and set it on the table. Russell pulled at Armand's arm and pulled him half out of the seat. "I wish to sleep. Go somewhere else."

"You're no fun." Armand got up all the same, picking up his glass and bottle of vodka with one hand. He pointed at Alfie with the index finger not holding the other two items. "Don't be like him."

Alfie remained tense until the man resettled next to his blonde compatriot, who herself hadn't moved an inch since the plane lifted off the ground. She was like a girl's toy doll, only creepier. Alfie slouched in his chair, rubbing his eyes under his glasses. He dropped his hand to his lap, looking over at Russell. "We don't have to follow them around or anything in Germany, do we?"

"No, but Armand is sort to leave with plane." Russell flexed his fingers in his lap. Armand pulled out a sleep-mask from his jacket and adjusted it over his head. The man crossed his arms and looked to have the same idea, but it could be an act as well. Russell was glad he had plenty of practice pulling all nighters. "Best to keep in sight at all time."

"That's what I figured." Alfie reached behind him and knocked back the seat rest. "I take it the sleep thing was a lie?"

"Yes," Russell said, amused. He pulled out his book, and settled into his chair. "But you sleep."

"Might as well," Alfie said closing his eyes, curling into his side. "Not much else to do."

Russell closed his book and set it on the seat next to him. He yawned into his hand, and rolled his shoulder. Across from him, Alfie slept, slouched against the side wall of the plane. He had crawled across the second seat in his sleep to get more comfortable, however, the angle of his neck suggested his attempt ended in failure. Russell searched the overhead compartment for a pillow, but found nothing but empty space in the small area. He clicked open the compartment next to it, as Armand's Keeper walked up behind him.

Duchess tapped Russell on the shoulder, holding out a square pillow and a plush blanket. He took it with a nod of thanks, and she went back to her side of the plane shaking her head. She pulled down another pillow and blanket set from the top compartment for her own sleeping charge. Duchess propped Armand into a better position, he too having slouched uncomfortably, and covered him with the blanket. She finished by adjusting his sleep-mask back into place over his eyes.

Along the same mindset, Russell gently lifted Alfie's head, and placed the pillow beneath it. He barely had time to finish draping the blanket before Alfie grabbed it in his sleep, snuggling into it. Russell sat back down, and covered his mouth with his fingers to hold back the yawn. He could use the rest himself, having been up solid since Alfie discovered what was wrong with his computer. However, there was still—

Duchess appeared at his side again, hands on her hips. She mimed sleeping with two hands clasped together near the side of her head. Russell made a move to speak, but she shushed him with an index finger to her lip. Duchess brushed a bit of hair to the side of Alfie's face with a soft smile, and backed up to point at Russell. She mimed the "sleep" motion again, and went back to her seat. She pointed at her eyes with two fingers, and then pointed them at the sleeping Armand. She pointed at Russell again, and once more mimed the "sleep" motion, followed by a thumbs up.

Russell let out a breath, and sunk into the leathery seat. Duchess would watch Armand for him. She may be as brutal as Armand when she wanted to be, but Duchess was far more trustworthy. The woman had the patience and control to rival saints, even able to stand at attention longer than Russell without the littlest twitch. She was the perfect Keeper for Armand, and as such, Russell could trust her to keep watch. He relaxed his muscles and closed his eyes. He was used to pulling days without sleep, but you never turned down rest when you could get it.

As Russell settled down for sleep he much clearly needed, Duchess returned to her seat, smiling knowingly at her partner. She tapped him in the leg with the tip of her shoe.

Armand lifted his eye-cover up an inch to get a good look at the sleeping pair down the plane aisle. Duchess pulled out her miniature digital notebook and started to type. Armand shifted in his seat, and yawned, removing the blanket and pillow. Duchess flipped her screen around, and he glanced at the message written across the screen:

> *Russell really likes this one. Think Sam'll be out of a job?*

"Don't know," Armand whispered. He drummed his fingers over his lips, turning in his seat to look at the big brute and his diminutive little tag-a-long. "But he is pretty over-protective. Maybe Ruskie doesn't want me offing the kid before he finds his targets."

Duchess shook her head and typed. She tapped Armand on the shoulder and forced him to read the screen.

> *No, he wants to be friends with that boy. I can tell.*

"Women's intuition?"

> *Yes. It's never failed me before.*

Duchess rubbed her bottom lip, with a silent giggle. Her finger came back clean, and she reminded herself to wear her lipstick tomorrow. Maybe pink. Duchess crossed her legs, and bit her bottom lip.

> *Alfie's pretty cute. I hope he's a keeper.*

"That was an awful pun, Duch." Armand crossed one knee over the other, mirroring his companion. He pulled out a folded knife from his pocket, and flicked the blade out. He pointed it at the woman grinning at him. "And your taste is awful."

> *Oh, like you don't think he's cute, too. I saw the way you looked at him over there. You even impressed him with a cherry stem. I don't blame you, though. He's like a puppy.*

Armand flipped the blade back into the knife's handle, and released it again. He repeated the action as Russell slept soundly across the room, legs stretched out across the gap and resting on the other side's arm rests like an early warning system. Armand wouldn't deny it though, people like Russell getting that personally involved made people like little Alfie infinitely more interesting. Russell hadn't been this attached to someone since he got partnered up with Sam.

Armand flicked the knife open again. "I like to skin puppies."

Duchess shrugged her shoulders, and dropped her leg back down. She crossed her ankles as she typed:

> *Same thing.*

CHAPTER 5

RUSSELL AND ALFIE dumped their bags in a hotel room located somewhere in scenic Munich. From the window, Alfie could see a huge park and some cathedrals, but heck if he knew what any of them were called. They looked distinct enough to be easily looked up on his computer with a quick search, but then Alfie reconsidered when he remembered he was essentially on what was an assassination trip. He decided the less he knew about anything the better. Plausible deniability was far more convincing when he was being honest about not having a clue where he was, or where they took him.

And also much easier to claim he was kidnapped.

Alfie rubbed the back of his neck as Russell smoothed the bedsheets out on the bed (only one, to Alfie's internal distress) humming something soft. A lullaby, maybe? Alfie wasn't sure, but it was a soothing melody coming from such a sturdy man. Alfie slipped his carrier bag off his shoulder and let it drop between the bed and the tiny nightstand. He heard Armand giving Duchess orders through the paper-thin wall of the attached room next to their suite, reinforcing Alfie's belief that Armand was unable to keep his mouth shut for any given amount of time while he was awake. Their hit was scheduled for sometime tomorrow morning, and Russell assured Alfie he would hear if the two tried to sneak out early.

Alfie collapsed onto the bed, a puff of dust surrounding him. For such an opulent ride in, they were pinching pennies when it came to their hotel. This place was more ramshackle than Alfie's apartment, but still managed to be more furnished than Russell's. Specifically, side-tables and lamps. Granted, he wasn't sure having more rats, cockroaches, or decaying furniture pieces was an improvement or not, but at least it felt more lived in. Alfie pulled himself back up and groped over the side for his computer bag. At least one thing could feel like home in this dump.

On the other side of the bed, Russell fluffed a pillow in a desperate attempt to make it usable. The filth around them disgusted him, and every inch of his skin shivered in desire to clean, but Russell would preserver. Just over the stained off-white sheet, he could see Alfie lean over the bed and scoot the side table over. Russell pulled back the bedspread to see equally filthy sheets under the comforter. A roach scurried across the surface looking for the return of its dark hiding spot, and he replaced the covers back down without hesitation.

Russell would be sleeping on top of the blankets.

He tucked the edges of the comforter under the mattress as Alfie let out a hushed expletive. Russell placed the pillow back on the bed, and asked, "What is wrong?"

"I didn't bring any adapters." Alfie held up his laptop power cord to show off his worthless plug. How he could have let something so important slip his mind? Different country, different voltage, was Rule #1 for the computer tech on the go. Alfie tossed the cord on the bed. "No electricity for me."

Russell placed his bag on the floor and checked his watch. Alfie did not have time to play on the computer anyway if they hoped to get enough sleep in for their big day tomorrow. They'd both need to be awake and alert if they wanted to keep track of Armand, while avoiding him at the same time. But, the other man looked upset, so it wouldn't hurt to feign interest. It was how nine out of ten of his conversations with Sam started, anyway. Russell lifted the edge of the cord and tapped the silver prong on the end as Alfie packed his things back up. "I do not understand. Why this not work?"

"Europe uses different voltages than the United States." Alfie zipped his messenger bag with his computer stowed away, hoping to preserve what little battery life his laptop had left for an emergency. The zipper didn't close all the way and he looked up at the cord still on the bed. "I'd need a 120 volt adapter to plug it in. We could buy one in town, I suppose, but we won't be here long, right?"

"Will this be problem in Lithuania?" Russell asked, turning the cord over in his hand. This is why he preferred more mechanical things. A club or gun was the same no matter where you were. Russell dropped

Alfie's power cord back on the bed. He would consent that the ammunition changed depending what you were using, but that was far easier to keep track of than electrical voltages in a country. Russell pointed at the end of the cord as it disappeared into a coil, and was stuffed into the bag with the laptop. "You will need, yes?"

"It's possible they have the same voltage as Germany, but since I don't know for sure it'd be best to just get one there." Alfie crawled back on the bed, hoping their shower worked in the morning. His clothes were clean, but he could use a bar of soap to at least attempt to scrub away all the fear-driven sweat he'd accumulated over the past day or so. He toppled onto his back, and his nose scrunched coming in contact with the cloud of dust again. He might need a change of clothes, too. Alfie covered his eyes with his arms and pretended he was at home. "If all else fails, I can charge it on the plane."

Russell laid down on his half of the bed, lying side by side with the programmer. Alfie stiffened in place when their arms brushed, and Russell moved over an inch away from him. Alfie relaxed, and Russell considered that a victory. On undercover nights like this, he and Sam would often get stuck sharing a queen or king as single-bed rooms were cheaper. Sam didn't know the meaning of staying still, and would often find six or eight positions during the night before he stopped rolling around. Russell was used to being hit by a stray limb, slept on, or flat out drooled on while he slept. Alfie remained motionless, as still as Russell on his side of the bed.

It was an odd sort of comfort to have a still, yet breathing, body next to him.

Russell heard Armand getting ready for bed in the other room, his constant murmurs to Duchess getting lighter and farther apart. He drifted off to the soothing mixture of Armand's voice over Alfie's light breathing. The ceiling above them was cracked, the plaster spreading and weaving in fine web-like patterns. The room had no overhead lamp, and the light at his side flickered through the heavy smell of dust. Russell switched it off, bathing them both in darkness, only a sliver of light spilling onto the floor through a crack in the blinds. Russell crossed his arms on his chest, listening to the sounds of four people breathing.

Sleep pulled at Alfie, even in the dank, foul smelling room; tiredness winning over fear. His breath evened, and even Russell a few inches away didn't register on his subconscious any longer.

"About tomorrow," Russell said, speaking up suddenly in the dark. He rubbed his fingers across his knuckles. "We follow Armand, but you not need to watch."

"Sounds good to me," Alfie mumbled. He turned facing the wall, wrinkling his nose in the film of dirt covered pillow. He sneezed into it, and curled further into himself getting as much warmth from his arms as possible without the blanket. If Russell didn't want to climb under the covers, Alfie had a feeling that he didn't either. Even in the chill, though, his body felt heavy like he was sinking into the mattress. "Wasn't going to, anyway."

Russell wanted to pat the boy on the shoulder goodnight, like he would do for Sam, but stopped his hand short mid-air. Instead, he cupped his hands back together over his chest, and closed his eyes. Alfie was not Sam, and they were not friends. They were business associates at most. Russell counted the cracks in the ceiling for ten seconds before closing his eyes.

Alfie and Russell woke a moment later to the groaning of Armand next door.

Armand's panting declarations of love and beauty, though poetic, still managed to sound obscene through the plaster. Each spoken word was accented by the creaking of an aged mattress and the whine of worn springs.

Alfie rolled over on his stomach toward Russell and ripped the pillow off the bed to shove it on top of his head and over his ears. Alfie's side was flush with the larger man's, but he didn't care. He merely pretended the insect that crawled out from underneath the pillow didn't exist, and squeezed his eyes shut. Alfie sucked in a deep breath of stale air, and clamped the pillow harder to his head in a desperate attempt to block out the noise. Russell sunk deeper into the bed beside him, sighing heavily.

At least they had that in common.

The wall shook with a thump, followed by a second that sounded suspiciously like a fist pounding into the plaster. A deep, needy moan came right after, only hidden by the renewed bed creaking.

Russell removed his pillow with one hand and held it over his head. He dropped it, the fabric plopping onto his face. As the mushroom cloud of dust settled, Russell thanked anyone that would listen to his thoughts that at least Sam wasn't there to commentate.

Alfie jumped out of the cold shower shivering, launching himself toward the moss-green towel hanging on the sidewall. How Russell managed to take a shower in the arctic-like temperatures without so much as a flinch, he'd never know. It probably came as a bundle deal with his lessons on standing still and looming menacingly. Alfie, on the other hand, had yelped like a puppy getting its tail pulled (Armand laughed at him through the wall) the second the frigid water smacked into his back. Under normal circumstances, he would have forgone the shower. Sharing a bed with cockroaches, sweat, and the grimy feeling one gets after listening to someone else have sex, however, bypassed "normal" long ago.

Alfie wanted that shower.

Russell was in the process of pulling down his shirt when Alfie walked back into the main room with the dingy towel around his waist. The computer tech stopped dead, and almost checked his pulse for shock. Alfie had been wrong when he first met the blond. The shirt *did* hide that man's muscles. *Russell's ripped as a tank*, Alfie thought as perfect pecs disappeared behind a black turtleneck. Alfie pulled his towel tighter and higher to hide his soft belly. He wasn't fat or anything, but there was a distinct lack of muscle definition that made him rush to drag on his own clothes.

Alfie buttoned his shirt when Armand let himself into the room, spitting perfection in a tailored grey suit. His hair was combed, his teeth were cleaned, and he looked like he just stepped out of a five-star hotel instead of the dingiest place they could find in Munich. Duchess followed, equally pressed and spit-spot. Not a hair was out of place from her short bangs to the pony-tail on top of her head. Her cat-pin had been traded out for a small sparrow with green eyes, and she was sporting cherry-red lipstick today. Alfie rushed through the last of his buttons. Neither of them looked liked they'd spent two or three hours last night making dents in the wall.

"You guys ready for breakfast?" Armand asked, leaning against the doorway. He smoothed back his hair, letting a few strands hang free from the style, and fixed his eyebrows. He primped like a peacock, and didn't care who knew it. "I know I am."

"Will be down," Russell said, sitting on the bed to gather his shoes. Armand and Duchess stayed in the doorway, watching Alfie. Russell pointed at the door as he held his shoe, laces undone. "Go."

"Fine, fine," Armand held up his hands, and turned around. Russell glared harder, and Armand chuckled as he stepped fully out of the doorway. He shoved his hands into his pockets and leaned back on his heels for a second before straightening. "Heaven forbid we walk down together."

Alfie shoved his feet into his own shoes, as Russell tied his laces methodically. Armand and Duchess left, both of their shoes clacking on the hardwood floor. As her blonde ponytail disappeared from view, Alfie put his hands in his pocket. Curiosity was a nasty temptress. He whispered, "So, what's the deal with those two? They an item or something?"

"No," Russell said. He grabbed his bag and set it on the bed, before rolling his shoulders back. Russell folded his clothing around the weapons as a cushion to better secure them for the upcoming day trip. It was Armand's job, so he really didn't need to be prepared for anything but watching today. Besides, he had his fists for weapons if something came up unexpectedly. Russell reached over for Alfie's bag and packed that up as well. "Duchess is like Sam. Armand is just high maintenance."

"Sam?" Alfie picked up his messenger bag and secured it over his shoulder. There was not a chance he was leaving his bag in this apartment. Russell started to throw Alfie's used clothes in the duffle bag, and Alfie went into the bathroom to retrieve his toiletries. He tossed them in the bag right after and looked at the pile of bags on the bed. Looked like they were taking all their things on this trip. "You said Sam was your partner, right?"

"Yes, Sam is my Keeper." Russell grabbed both packs and tossed them over his shoulder. He waved his hand in the air as if it would explain in more detail for him. "Like Duchess is Armand's Keeper. I say this."

Alfie sat on the edge of the bed He rubbed his fingers in the rough fabric of the blanket. "You're losing me with this 'Keeper' thing you keep mentioning."

"Ah, when I do job, I get…what is word?" Russell tapped his finger on the edge of the bag strap. "Distracted? In over head? Sam is grounding. I see Sam, I remember job and what I am doing. Duchess is same for Armand. Sex is either perk, or control method. Hard to tell with them. Armand is wild card. Sometimes he needs distracting when off-duty. High maintenance."

Alfie slid the clasp on his strap up and down. He thought of the girl-obsessed man who overloaded his servers on a monthly basis and had Alfie on speed dial it seemed like. Alfie frowned, pinching his brows together. Sam almost never left his house, and yet he was following Russell around all the time? "And Sam does that stuff for you? The bringing back to reality and distracting stuff? He doesn't seem the responsible type."

"He is not. I babysit *him*." Russell opened the door, shaking his head. Sam required twenty-four hour attention when they were on a job. He liked to touch things, or say things, or just plain make a mess. It was like he had no sense of self-preservation. Alfie was not so bad, but at the moment his ignorance of the job and place was sticking him in a similar bracket. Questioning about Armand and Duchess when they could probably still hear him through the wall being one of them. "Like I do for you now, and why Sam is not here. You are his replacement for this trip."

"Joy for me." Alfie followed him out the door, a frown working on his face. He wasn't sure what was more insulting, being a replacement for Sam or implying that he was as much trouble as Sam. "But I definitely don't need baby—"

"Better distraction from bloodlust than sex," Russell interrupted. He pushed Alfie out the door and into the hallway toward the rickety stairs. The plaster flaked off the walls as they shook the floorboards walking. "Now go. I am hungry. You too, yes?"

Alfie ignored the creaking under his feet and the vertigo that the floor was about to fall out from under him any second. "Sure, why not. What's bloodlust without a little breakfast?"

"Now you get it," Russell said, grinning and slapping the boy on the back.

Breakfast was an awkward affair with chocolate eyes grinning in constant amusement at a blushing Alfie and a frowning Russell. Alfie bit into a thin biscuit, the bread crisp and heavily buttered. The café served coffee and a variety of baked goods, so at least there were distractions abound for the nervous programmer as he avoided agitating "Wild Card" Armand, and tried to contemplate his role as "Keeper of the Day." He had apparently been doing so without knowing before, so was he supposed to act differently now that he knew? Alfie was tempted to text

Sam and ask him what he was missing in this equation.

Russell finished his food last, and nursed a cup of coffee while he waited on Armand to get moving. Seeing neither of them touching their plates, he pushed up from the table after setting the empty dish aside. Alfie grabbed his things and followed the cue along with Duchess and Armand. It looked like it was time to get this show on the road, bellies full and minds set.

There was just one little problem.

"What do you mean he's not going to watch?" Armand whined around a bite of a pastry he snatched from a waiter's tray as they left the café. He licked his thumb and pouted to the best of his ability. "You must be joking."

Alfie looked back and forth between Armand and Russell as he trotted alongside them. Duchess followed, her ponytail swishing back and forth from the top of her head as she dragged hers and Armand's luggage behind her. He figured it was for the same reason Russell was carrying theirs, and why he had his bag. No one trusted their stuff in that dingy hotel, even if it was a block from where they were eating. Their breakfast location was also only a few buildings down from their target's hideaway, allowing them easy access to the target's location.

Alfie wondered if Armand's "play thing," as he put it, had any clue they were coming. It was doubtful considering they chose a hotel location, and ate food out in the open, less than a five minute walk around the corner. However, that was the least of Alfie's concerns at the moment with the look Armand was giving him.

"That is completely unfair of you." Armand shoved the last bit of cinnamon goodness into his mouth, and wiped his fingers on a handkerchief from his pocket. He shoved it back in with a huff. He pointed at Alfie and waved his hand in Russell's face. "I finally have an audience unfamiliar with my work, and you're snatching him away, Ruskie!"

"Not a Russian." Russell followed the man, wearing his turtleneck and jeans, bags tapping at his side as he carried them. Much more practical to Armand and Duchess' suits. Alfie followed in almost as sensible light blue polo and khakis, his knees shaking behind the fabric. "Alfie not in group. He does not need to see."

Armand turned on his heel, and walked down the street backwards. He focused in on Alfie, putting one hand on his chest over his heart. He would appeal to the boy's curiosity. Surely he would want to watch! It was the chance of a lifetime, and Armand was nothing but entertaining. "You want to watch me, don't you? I'm an artist, not like that brute. I can promise you'll enjoy every second of my work."

Alfie took a step back and knocked into Russell as Armand leaned in. Chocolate eyes pleaded with him, doing their best impression of a demented puppy. Alfie held his hands up in his defense, wanting to deflect Armand before he turned into the raging guard dog everyone seemed to hint that he could be. "If it's all the same, I think I'll just wait outside with Russell."

"I insist you come in." Armand clamped a hand on the slighter man's shoulder, halting both of them in their tracks. He never got to show off in front of a real audience. Duchess and Russell were capable of the same, if not worse and they were (quite frankly) often *bored* watching. That wasn't good enough for Armand.

Terrified faces and the whites of people's eyes were the best part of this job. The twisted, crooked transformation of innocent skin into horrified screaming when nothing had yet touched them was a delicacy. He just *knew* this Alfie's face would be exquisite and he had to see it; the preview he was getting right now was enough to get his blood pumping in anticipation. Alfie's eyebrows had dropped, and his mouth had formed a grimace. Combined with the tension in his shoulders and the shaking under Armand's palm, it was almost too much.

Armand was an exhibitionist through and through. Guilty as the day he was born. Alfie needed to watch. Armand squeezed his hold. "You can't come all this way and not get a little blood on those nice clean pants of yours."

"That's really okay." Alfie took a step back, yanking his arm free from Armand. He hid behind Russell's bicep, rubbing his arm where Armand had gripped it. He had called Russell crazy over a day ago to Sam on the phone, but he was starting to realize that Russell was the sane one in this party. Besides, Russell liked him, which was a little disturbing, but even scarier was that Alfie was starting to get the vibe that Armand liked him, too. "I'll just sit it out. I might make a fool of myself and embarrass you. You wouldn't want that, right?"

"No, don't be absurd." Armand stuck his hand in his pocket. "You couldn't embarrass me. I'm a professional and I absolutely insist that you come in and watch."

"Armand, he is not watching." Russell took a protective step further in front of Alfie, forcing Armand to back off. He stood a good head and a half taller than Armand Dubois, and used it. "My charge. My rules."

"I will cut him." Armand flipped open his switchblade, the red handle and shining silver blade glistening in the midday sun. His face contorted into a vicious snarl, eyes wide and mad. Armand pointed the knife at Alfie, whose face had gone a delicious shade of milk-white. "No, I take that back. I will stab him. I will take this knife, and shove it straight through his Adam's Apple until it comes out the other side and he's choking on his own blood in the middle of the sidewalk!"

"What?" Alfie asked, his voice rattled. A hand clamped down on his wrist, and he saw Duchess smiling at him calm and pleasant as if they were shopping in a department store. She had him trapped under her well manicured, pink-polished nails. Alfie twisted his arm to loosen her grip and escape her hold. Her tiny form didn't budge an inch, so Alfie went with bargaining. "You don't really want to do that, do you?"

"I will very much want it." Armand stalked around the brute until he was in Alfie's face. Russell tensed and readied to grab Armand not more than a foot away. "So I'll say it again: If you don't watch me work, this is going in your throat and you will die as painfully as I can make it.

"And don't you think little Ruskie will help. I kill you, and the worst he can do in retaliation is kill me." Armand stepped around Russell, and tapped Alfie on the side of the cheek with the blade edge. Russell growled under his breath, but Armand wasn't deterred. He shifted it so that the point dented the skin without breaking it. "Which he won't, because there's no way he'll survive killing the Boss' best hit man and he knows it. Killing an insignificant pet of his would not even begin to be a good enough excuse."

"Let him go, Armand." Russell said, his voice gravely with anger. The man had a point, and Alfie's innocence to the world of tortures wasn't worth all of them dying. Russell grabbed Armand's lapel and pulled him away from the little Keeper-in-Training. "He will watch."

"See? That wasn't so hard!" Armand pushed Russell's arm off of him, smoothing out his suit. He flipped his knife back into it's folded position, and secured it away in his pocket. Armand grinned his million-watt smile, and smoothed his expression back down from enraged maniac to playboy in a blink. His blood started pumping faster in excitement. Their target was only a block away; his audience was ready. "This is going to be fantastic, you just wait. You won't regret it one little bit, Alfie."

Duchess released the young man's wrist the second Armand turned back around to continue their trek to the target's place. Alfie rubbed the bruised flesh, and stayed standing next to Russell as the two entered the nearest building as if nothing had happened.

Armand called out "Hurry along now!" before disappearing behind the door, Duchess quick on his heels with both suit cases.

Alfie rubbed his cheek where the blade had been moments before, his eyes wide and fingers dry. His body shook with tremors, and he was impressed he hadn't wet himself. Alfie felt a hand on his back and leaned into it. His lungs burned as he breathed. "What just happened?"

Russell rubbed Alfie's back with his thumb, soothing the shaking thing. The next few hours were not going to be pretty if he was going into shock from just a threat. "Armand had a fit."

"That happen often?" Alfie curled his arms in on himself, gripping his shoulder bag.

"Try and look afraid," Russell said. "He likes it."

"Oh, trust me. There won't be any trying." Alfie whined, feeling his heartbeat get ahead of him. "Genuine fear, right here."

Armand worked fast.

Russell and Alfie trudged up the apartment stairs, as rickety and creaking as the ones in their own hotel. Alfie watched each step, his weight threatening to snap each board as he climbed. The brick walls felt like they were falling in on him, and the chipped paint on the blue doors held no comfort. They reached the top landing sooner than they'd like, to see their appointed room door hitched open by Duchess.

She stood in the hallway, like a doorman waiting for his master to come home complete with a hand on her waist. Duchess wore a doll's smile, fake and plastic. Her pin sat crooked on her lapel, but otherwise not a hair looked out of place. She held out her hand at Alfie when he got to the door, and he clutched at his messenger bag strap as he looked at Russell for some sort of cue.

"She wants bag," Russell said, dropping both of his own next to the suitcases stacked neatly in the hallway. He rolled up his sleeves to his elbows, hoping to spare at least some of the fabric even if the shirt would be a lost cause. Cut off sleeves made for great cleaning rags. Russell tugged on Alfie's computer bag strap. "Armand is messy."

"She's not coming in?" Alfie asked, clinging to his bag like a lifeline. If Duchess wasn't going in—what if Russell wasn't going in either? Alfie wasn't going in alone with Armand was he? He grabbed Russell's rolled sleeve in his fist, aware that his breath and heart rates were elevating in a miniature panic attack. "You're coming in, too, right?"

"Yes, I am coming, too," Russell said, his lips tugging into an inappropriate smile. He patted Alfie on the head once for comfort, and then dropped his arms. Russell took in a deep breath and rolled his shoulder, making sure to be stretched and prepared for anything. "Armand works alone, but he likes to be watched. You and I are audience, so Duchess is not needed."

"Lucky Duchess." Alfie handed over his bag, extending his arm as if he were approaching a lion rather than a lady. The purpled bruise on his wrist was the only reminder he needed that she was a also a petite powerhouse. Duchess took the bag before his hand made it to her, and set it neatly on the floor with the rest of their things. Alfie took the more genuine smile that spread across her face and her extended arm past the doorway as his cue to go in.

Alfie stood in front of the doorway like it was a passage way to his inevitable death. How did he get from hunting cyber criminals, to sitting in with blood-thirsty, trigger happy serial-killers?

Really, Universe. Alfie would like that answered at some point.

Russell pushed Alfie forward, his feet crinkling on some sort of waxy paper that lined the floor and worked its way up the walls. Yellowed newspapers crinkled beneath that, the paper brittle and cracking under each footstep. His cautious pace on the creaking wood of the floor brought Alfie no comfort, unsure if the boards would hold either of them up. If you replaced the putrid shade of lime green that decked the walls with an off-white you'd have the spitting image of the hotel they stayed in last night, only worse. Russell kept to his back, making sure, once again, that Alfie didn't make a spontaneous, fear-driven run for it. He wasn't sure if it was reassuring or not that Russell had his back.

Literally in this case.

Dead center in the room, stood Armand and someone strapped to a chair with leather belts around her legs and arms. Alfie jerked to a stop when he realized their target wasn't some big hit-man thug like Russell, or a slimly charismatic like Armand. But instead, she was a nineteen or twenty year old woman with pale, smooth skin under the smudged makeup. Her auburn hair was frazzled and pulled halfway out of a scrunchie like someone had grabbed her by it. She was a bit heavier than most women Alfie knew, but it was a sturdy sort of weight—muscles and girth under taut skin. Her eyes were wide in fear, the hazel irises almost engulfed by her dilated pupils.

"Do not be fooled." Russell whispered in his ear. Alfie jumped in surprise, and Russell had to grab his shoulders to hold him steady. He kept his eyes on the woman in the center of the room, and the too widely grinning Armand. Bethany was dressed down in a grey jumpsuit with white pinstripes. Her hack around clothes. The zipped hoodie hung open and her tank-top undershirt was stained with tiny specks of blood from a previous engagement. Russell was no more going to take his eyes off of her than he was Armand. "She is great killer. Bigger list than mine and Armand put together."

"Which is why I'm so very, very glad she decided to betray the faction." Armand slapped her on the side of the face. Her head slammed to the side of the chair, mouth hitting the edge of the chair top. Half of him was disappointed he'd actually caught her off guard. It had been too easy to restrain her while she fixed her morning coffee. A pull on the hairpiece, a kick to her stomach from Duchess, and tied to a chair before the steam stopped rising from her coffee cup. It had taken less than five minutes. "I've always wanted dibs on Ms. Bethany, you know?"

"Because you're a monster, Dubois!" she said, spitting at the man's face. The glop dripped down his cheek, wetting his concealer. "I have a higher hit count, but that's only because I work faster than you!"

Armand wiped the wet spot from his face with a handkerchief. He took care putting it back in its place, face clean. He removed a slim compact from his back pocket, and touched up the offending spot with the included sponge. His make-up fixed, Armand drove his heel into the woman's stomach in the same motion that he replaced his touch-up kit in his pocket. She doubled over in her restraints, wheezing from the sharp kick. Armand smoothed his hair down. "Don't be rude, darling. We have guests, you know."

Alfie glued himself to Russell's side, shamelessly clutching his arm. The man was strong, unflinching, and the lesser of three evils in this room. Armand unrolled a case on the countertop with a single flick of his wrist, revealing a set of sharp scalpels, knives, and assorted dental picks. They gleamed, silver and sharp, reflecting the light from between the window's shutters. The same light covered Armand and his knives in a crisscross pattern that shadowed his eyes and lit up his smile.

Alfie may have whimpered.

Armand loved the sound of fear. His guest's face was an exquisite shade of grey, and the way he practically crawled inside of Ruskie to hide was the highlight of his week. Bethany was too fearless; too hardened to be affected by his talented hand. Russell's face was a stone statue even while he was working, so little Alfie was all he really had available to entertain. Armand selected his favorite scalpel from the set, the blade two inches thick. He heard Alfie's gasp, and it put a movie-star smile of glee on his face. "Let's not keep them waiting, shall we?"

Alfie made it until the blade had cut two inches into her neck before his knees gave out and Russell had to catch him under his arms to keep the poor programmer upright.

Two and a half excruciating hours later, Ms. Bethany was dead and there wasn't a dry spot on anyone in the room.

Alfie plucked the top of his shirt and held it out an inch. Russell's arms were still locked around his chest and waist in an oddly comforting hug that was the only thing keeping Alfie on his feet. The red soaked fabric was damp under Alfie's fingertips, and drips of the thick liquid in his hair rolled down the sides of his face. Droplets clung to his glasses, in beads and watery lines.

Alfie asked Russell, "This is why you only own like four outfits from discount stores, isn't it?"

"More or less." Russell shifted to hold Alfie up with one arm, and flicked his free hand to the side to remove the excess liquid. It was a wonder Armand never got caught. Alfie slumped into his side, legs lazy and long adjusted to Russell holding him up for the past couple of hours. Alfie's voice had given out an hour ago from the screaming, and he'd fallen into quiet shivering for the rest of the time. Russell was more relieved than he'd like to admit that Alfie still had the strength of mind to chat after watching all of that. "Only Armand waste money on good clothes."

"I have to look my best," Armand said, with an air of breathlessness. His heart rate crawled back to its normal tempo from the exhausting race of adrenaline and excitement it had suffered from a few moments before. He pulled a cigarette from his pocket and lit it up, sitting in the chair Ms. Bethany had previously occupied. She, in contrast, was currently sprawled across the floor. And on the bed. And a piece of her finger was in the far corner of the room on a stack of old fashion magazines. Armand sucked in a mouthful of smoke, relishing the post-coital bliss. "Otherwise I'd be a classless peon like the rest of you."

Russell let Alfie gently down to the floor, his knees splashing in a puddle of red. Once he was sure Alfie wasn't planning on moving any time soon, Russell walked to the back room and rummaged around for a towel or something to mop himself and Alfie up with. It took him five minutes of searching, but he eventually found a stack of clean towels in the kitchen. Russell dropped one on Alfie's head. He held the ends with both hands, but made no move to clean up or remove it from where it had fallen. Instead, Alfie pulled it tightly over his head like a hood. Russell rubbed the blood off his own hands, and sighed.

"No need for that, Ruskie." Armand shoved the lit end of the cigarette into the chair, extinguishing the flame and leaving a burn mark in the wood. His legs were limp, and he didn't feel like moving for a week. Armand couldn't remember the last time he had a job this utterly satisfying. "Duchess'll clean up."

Russell wetted the towel under the kitchen sink faucet anyway. He wiped off his face, and rinsed it again. Russell rubbed the towel into his hair and scrubbed. "You are sloppy, Armand."

"I'm an artiste! The room is my canvas, you know." Armand forced his limbs to wake up by slapping the top of his thighs. He knew better than to sit down after a job. Too easy to relax and bask in his art. Armand stood when the blood flow started again, and squished through the mess to the door. He stopped by the shivering Alfie Knight, and offered the man a cigarette. The boy took it, but let it hang in his hand next to the unused towel. Armand rubbed the man's hair through the terrycloth with both hands. He really had been a fantastic audience. Armand hadn't heard screaming like that in years. "Duchess has a change of clothes for all of us waiting outside, and the room next door was cleared for us to change if I'm not mistaken."

Alfie stumbled to his feet when Armand stopped touching him, catching himself on the wall. The towel and cigarette dropped to the ground, splashing in the muck. He waited for Russell to join him before following Armand into the hallway, eager for the promise of fresh clothes. His feet stuck to the sections of clean floor as he trailed blood behind him. Duchess handed him a tote he hadn't seen her with before. Alfie held it away from himself, to avoid covering it with Bethany's blood, too.

Alfie sighed as he rounded the corner, his shoulders drooping and his body sore. The room next door to the leftover carnage was clear of life save for Armand stripping. The older man swapped his clothes out for a new suit with a hum on his lips and a bit of bounce in his movements. The clothes hit the ground one at a time, revealing pale and scared skin. Alfie stood staring for a moment, before Russell passed by him and followed suit. Armand was as well built as Russell, though slimmer. Alfie compared openly, having lost all traces of bashfulness in the past few hours. All he wanted was something to wear not covered in the remains of another person.

Alfie dropped the bag of clothes on the bed as Armand and Russell finished changing behind him. He wiped his hands off on the few clean spots on his jeans, and unzipped the bag in a single clean swipe to poke through the contents. It contained a crisp white button up shirt, and black dress pants in Alfie's size, both by a name brand he couldn't pronounce. He lifted them out of the bag, and set them aside mechanically. Black dress shoes and socks were stuffed in the bottom, with a striped black and red patterned tie folded neatly on top. Silk. He reached for the tie, and caught sight of the sticky red substance still coating the back of his arm.

Alfie left the bag, choosing to wash his face and hands in the bathroom first. He turned on the sink for two seconds as the water splashed in the basin before turning it off again with a sharp twist of the handle. He stripped down to nothing, and jumped in the shower. He blasted the water, scalding hot by some miracle, and cleaned the blood from his hair and every inch that had seeped through his clothes. His movements were oddly calm and controlled as he used a dirty rag to scrub. He'd ran out of things to scream at watching Armand. Alfie turned the knob off and stepped out of the shower, shivering in the cold air. He retrieved his boxers, but left the rest of his clothes on the floor.

He dressed methodically, and before he knew it, Alfie wore clothes of a better quality than anything he'd ever owned in his twenty-six years of life. He smoothed the tie down in the mirror, admiring the cut of the outfit. It looked fitted. The lines hugged his body, making him look slimmer and better in shape than his slight roll of belly fat wrapped around his gut would attest. In this outfit, Alfie almost appeared like he belonged in Armand's crowd with pressed suits and double breasted jackets than with Russell and his usual turtleneck and jeans.

Speaking of his blond-headed giant, Russell walked behind him and tapped Alfie's shoulder. Armand headed out the door with an odd smirk on his face as he watched the two of them, and the young programmer gripped his pants leg. Russell shook his head and pushed Alfie toward the door. Time to go. Alfie laced up his shoes, and grabbed his computer bag before leaving the clean room behind. His clothes and Duchess' bag forgotten on the bed and bathroom floor, respectively. Alfie couldn't bring himself to care. He sucked in a deep breath, and tried to calm down. What was done was done, and he just had a few more days before he could go home and forget this entire ordeal.

Or at the very least track down the number to a good therapist.

The hallway was clear when they left the room, and the four took stock of their things. The building creaked around them, and the nauseating smell coming from the assassin's room made Alfie scrunch his nose.

"So," Alfie said, standing next to a cleaned Russell, resisting the urge to cover his nose or gag. Armand and Duchess were side by side across from them, Duchess sitting on the top of a suitcase. He made sure to face away from Bethany's previous room, and the sight of bloody footprints in the hallway. He really wanted to leave. Alfie rubbed his hands together. "Now what?"

"We get something to eat!" Armand slapped Russell and Alfie on the back, sidling up between them. He shifted his hands until his arms were around both of their shoulders. Armand held his hands there, and felt his energy returning with the trembling body under his right arm, and the annoyed one under his left. "By the time we're done, dear Duchess will have sanitized the rooms and we'll be ready to leave in the morning. Anyone have a preference? I'm thinking of visiting a favorite local spot, myself."

Russell removed Armand's hand and maneuvered Alfie free as well before pushing him to the front of the group. Russell ignored Armand's hurt look aimed in his direction, and instead focused on his charge. Alfie was still pale, but at least the tremors had stopped. Getting some food in his stomach was probably a good thing at this point. It would build his strength up. Distract him. Russell rubbed Alfie's back. "Food is good, yes?"

"Sure," Alfie said. "Food is good."

They were halfway through the main course when Duchess arrived.

Before that, Alfie had surprised himself by managing to eat everything that was placed in front of him without throwing up. His stomach almost appreciated the weight of the food. It settled him. Russell had even slipped him an extra roll of bread at some point that Alfie happily devoured.

Alfie was a good halfway through his spätzle and beef stew, when Duchess sat next to him, and across from Armand. Her hair was down, and her jacket top was quickly tossed over the back of her chair. Duchess' clean shirt was unbuttoned halfway down, revealing a peak at her ivory lace bra from the way the shirt half folded when she sat. Alfie had to look away when his face heated from the sight. What was it with all these people being ridiculously attractive!

Alfie dared another glance and in addiction to the open shirt, her sleeves were rolled up to her elbows. She opened the menu waiting for her on the table with happy shoulder roll and a lazy smile. It was the most casual Alfie'd seen her since they'd met, verging on the surreal at seeing the living doll looking so human.

Catching Alfie's blatant wide-eyed staring, Armand explained around a bite of potato with a cheeky smile and a wink. "Duchess enjoys clean up. It really relaxes her, you see?"

He didn't but Alfie nodded all the same, resisting every urge to scoot his chair around the the table edge and next to Russell. Duchess ruffled was more disturbing than Duchess clean cut and crisp. Alfie shoved another bite of stew and pasta in his mouth. If cleaning up blood and gore was what got the woman off, Alfie wanted nothing to do with it. But, it did explain why she and Armand were partners. Alfie swallowed his food, and looked hopefully up at the two men. "So, after this we go back to the hotel?"

"Yes, and then we hunt down your little cyber criminals, and what not." Armand sipped his Riesling, enjoying the crisp fruity blend. Local was really the way to go, and the quaint little Ma & Pa restaurant they'd invaded was the place to be. Dim lighting, seating for only twenty, and the best wine in Munich. Armand couldn't have asked for a better follow-up to a spectacular performance. He clicked his tongue on the roof of his mouth. "What did the rascals do again, Ruskie?"

Russell slammed his fists, still gripping the silverware, down on the table. A waitress in the back dropped a glass, startled by the exclamation. "Not a Russian!"

"Yes, yes. Same question applies, *Russell.*" Armand took another bite of his potato and sucked on the fork. He spoke around it, voice muffled by the metal. "What'd they do to get you all worked up? You're not one to take jobs on your own, or at least not ones that don't stem from Sam whispering ideas in your ear."

"They stole from me," Russell said, relaxing his shoulders.

Armand removed the fork and moved it in a little circle in the air. The man needed to learn how to elongate his sentences. Details were the important parts in this business. "How?"

"They wrote malware that loaded itself on his machine when he was browsing a website," Alfie said when Russell didn't answer for a minute. Aside from "they stole from me," Alfie was still fairly convinced that the larger man didn't understood the exact details of what had happened to him. "It opened a backdoor on his system that gave the authors complete control of his computer. They used that to get his passwords and other information necessary to infiltrate his bank accounts to transfer his money. It wasn't really targeted, and could have happened to anyone, honestly."

"How dreadfully impersonal." Armand tapped his fork down on the plate one tap after another. He licked his teeth, and his leant on his elbow on the table. He stabbed a piece of potato, the force cracking the plate underneath. "I support you completely, Ruskie."

Russell didn't bother with his usual rebuke. He was already upset, and if he said it one more time he would be shouting. The waitress was already avoiding their table now, and he rather liked the food here. Russell swallowed a bite of his meal. "I agree."

"And you hunted the culprits down?" Armand asked, shifting his fork so it pointed at Alfie. The boy flushed and jerked to attention in his seat.

"More or less," Alfie said. He looked down at his place and tried to concentrate on eating. "We'll probably still have to go door to door though. Looking up folks by their IP address isn't exactly an exact science."

"It's still impressive."

"It-it really isn't." Alfie turned his attention back down to the table, and away from the flattery. This situation was too normal; he couldn't forget what happened this morning. "I mean, like I said, they may not even be there when we arrive. Anything could happen."

"And that's what makes it all the more fun, isn't that right?" Armand asked Duchess.

She nodded, and pointed at what she wanted from the menu when the waitress asked for her order, standing about an arm's length away.

Alfie ate faster, hoping to get the next part of his week over with.

Russell dumped their bags onto the bed of a much nicer hotel than the hovel they had used from before. The fountain in the main lobby being the biggest hint to the quality, in addition to the clean white linens and shampoo samples left in the shower. However, the lack of expensive and gaudy decorations everywhere, was his hint that Duchess chose the location over Armand. Russell would be the last to complain over the more sensible location choice.

Alfie collapsed face first on the bed, grumbling into the fabric about bad luck. Their plane was reporting a technical error of some sort when they arrived, so it couldn't take off for another two days. Alfie pulled the pillow into his face and rolled over onto his back. That left the four of them with nothing to do but sightsee in Munich.

Armand and Duchess had already run off on their own to who knows where, claiming they'd make it back in time for the plane. Theoretically they had a room adjoining to his and Russell's, but he doubted they actually spent any time in there.

That left Russell and Alfie alone, but with a much nicer budget. Alfie rolled over onto his side, arms wrapped stubbornly around the thick pillow. Russell had explained that cheap hotels helped the mood for a job, as well as made them much less conspicuous. Alfie argued someone in their organization would know something like that already, but he shrugged. Russell said there were many more cheap hotels in the world than expensive ones. Much easier to hide, either way.

Russell still only ordered a room with one bed though.

Alfie clicked the light on next to the bed, and then clicked it off. This lamp cost more than the crystal glasses on the plane. How on earth could you afford a room this nice and not be able to afford at least a room with a pull-out couch?

Russell sat on the opposite edge of the bed, listening to the click of the light going on and off. He pulled his phone out and stared at the screen. Alfie was bored, and Russell had no idea what to do with him for two days. At night they could sleep, but doing nothing but staring at each other all day would be uncomfortable for the both of them. If Sam were here, Russell would have no problem following along as the loud man "lived it up" in town. Restaurants, tourist things, and people watching were his forte.

Russell was much better at standing silently behind Sam and making sure he didn't get himself killed than coming up with his own things to do.

Alfie was an entirely different matter. He was quiet, calm, and most importantly, still jumpy around Russell. It was doubtful he'd take the lead for future activities.

Russell's phone buzzed, and he glanced down at the screen. Sam's text read:

You scare Alfie to death yet?

Followed by a quick second:

He's fragile.

Russell glanced behind him to the man who had given up on the lamp and pillow, and now had his face covered with his arms. Pouting. In long run, pouting was preferable to fear, but all the same something needed to done. Russell typed back:

I noticed. We have free time. What does he like to do?

It was a few moments before Russell received a response, which was no surprise. Sam and distractions went together like wine and cheese. When Russell did hear the chime of an answer, he could hear the indifference in his Keeper's tone through the text alone.

Work? I don't know. He's just my computer guru, man.

Russell clicked his phone shut. Sam was proving useless, as per usual. Why were they partners again? Russell shoved his phone in his pocket and stood. They were in Germany, in a large city, with plenty of things to do. There was no point in staying cooped up in here when they could at the very least take a walk around town. Surely the other man had something he had thought about wanting to do in Europe. Russell would just ask Alfie, and then get them both out of the room.

Alfie had a minor heart attack when a strong grip removed the arms from his face and he saw Russell looming above him. To his relief, it only managed to show on his face as minor shock. "Something up?"

"You and me. Go out."

"O-okay." Alfie slid off the bed and grabbed his computer bag. Russell was already out the door and he had to jog to keep up. "Where are we going?"

"Walk," Russell said. He glanced down at the younger man, and shifted from one foot to the other. "We can stop if you see something you like."

Alfie stood in the doorway staring for a few moments, before jogging to catch up to the flushing man. *Was Russell trying to be nice?*

Two days flew by faster than Alfie would have thought possible. Russell was strangely good company during his off hours when he wasn't plotting murder. Pleasant and quiet jumped straight to mind when thinking about him. Alfie would stop and shop, or look at some tourist sight that caught his eye as they wandered around town, and Russell followed. But that didn't mean he didn't pay attention. Russell was sort of like a giant guard dog.

Alfie had honestly never felt safer wandering around a foreign country.

They visited shops and whatever else caught their fancy as they trailed down the streets. For the most part, Alfie rather enjoyed his impromptu vacation. He'd even collected a variety of little gifts and trinkets to take home, all tucked away neatly in a new bag that Russell didn't mind carrying, and Alfie didn't have to pay for a thing. He supposed there were some perks to being kidnapped by rich people, even if they were criminals.

And Alfie supposed they weren't all bad.

Russell was a quiet companion, but made remarks when they were appropriate. Little observations, and even a joke once in a while came out of his mouth more often than Alfie would have thought. The big scary guard dog had a puppy side when he was happy. Russell opened up more and more the longer they were together, and Alfie found himself smiling more often than not right back in response during discussions.

He didn't even mind having to share a bed any longer by the second night.

It almost seemed too soon when Russell said they'd be boarding the plane in the morning, and Alfie went to sleep remembering the whole point of them being out here.

They were going to kill people.

Alfie pulled the sheets up to his eyes, and rolled onto his side. People were going to die like that Bethany girl.

His stomach lurched.

Alfie's good time for the past days left his head in a blur, replaced by thoughts he did not want. He threw off the covers, holding his hand over his mouth to stop the bile from bubbling up. Alfie pushed his way into the bathroom, and gratefully made it to the toilet when he emptied his stomach into the bowl. Alfie's stomach heaved as he vomited, visions of red and Armand laughing as he worked filling his head.

That had only been two days ago.

How was Alfie ever going to forget that? He'd shoved it from his mind for the past couple of days running around Munich with Russell, but it was still there at the corner of his mind. Denial only went so far, and Alfie couldn't take this. It was wrong. There had been so much blood, and she had screamed so much, and Armand! It was so, so wrong and—

Alfie threw up again.

He rested his head against the side of the toilet and whined. What had he gotten himself into? Was he really going to have to go through that again? And this time it would be Russell's turn. Alfie paled, thinking of the giant man. Would Russell be as bad as Armand? Worse?

"It is alright," Russell said from behind Alfie.

Russell knelt down next to Alfie and wiped away the bile from the edges of his lips off with a warm, damp rag. After cleaning Alfie's face, he flushed the toilet and lifted Alfie off the floor with the same ease that he carried around their luggage.

Alfie didn't struggle, leaning on Russell's chest and sighing when he was placed back onto the bed. Russell helped him under the covers again, and patted his side.

"Go to sleep," Russell said. "We leave early."

Alfie nodded, and rolled onto his side to hug the pillow. He pretended he didn't feel better when Russell kept rubbing his shoulder as he tried to pass out.

It was almost over.

They'd be done soon.

He'd just have to forget.

Alfie fell asleep to Russell's humming lullaby, and the gentle massage of his hand. How could someone about to do things so horrible, be so gentle?

CHAPTER 6

ROSS LEANED OVER his desk, eyes staring at the screen. The screams and shouted explicative words of their neighbors fighting next door echoed through the open window while he worked. It was distracting, but Ross didn't mind so much. Despite the hour of the night, he wasn't asleep, and besides, it's not like he understood what they were saying anyway.

His partner in crime didn't seem to mind much either.

Kirk typed away like a madman at his machine. Lines of code flying by, both new and revised, assaulted his senses in sweet bliss. It was beauty in motion. This project was going to change the world. Total access to everything he could ever want. Back doors, decryptions, hidden files, the works. A one-stop shop to more information and money than they could ever handle. Banks, personal computers, government, local—wouldn't matter. Kirk would get in without a trace, and leave with everything. Their *FlowerMantis69* would be an appetizer to this bad boy's main dish.

Kirk had never been prouder of his work.

While his partner crowed to himself, Ross transferred the last remaining funds from someone's second bank account. He typed slow, one key at a time as he activated the Husband command. Ross slunk in his seat, focusing on the shouting from the window and Kirk's rapid typing. His mouth was pressed in a firm line, and his back itched.

"What's bothering you, Ross?" Kirk asked, mid line. He was so close to finishing he could feel it in his blood, but it was hard to concentrate when his partner was over there dragging down his creative spirit. "You're acting like your mom died over there."

"It's that message, man." Ross shoved his keyboard away from him. He dropped his elbows on the desk, and rubbed at the side of his temples. The words blinked back at him behind closed eyelids. "I can't get it out of my head."

"The guy who said he'd break us?" Kirk snorted, hitting the Enter key. "Please, it was a bluff. Big guy acting all tough because he couldn't get to us. He's probably some little ninety pound dork who can't keep his glasses on."

"I don't know," Ross said. Their computer screens lit the dark room, bathing them both in blue. It was true that the internet was full of big-talkers and fakers, but there were some dangerous people hiding behind usernames, too. Ross rubbed his upper arm, feeling a chill despite the many servers whirling and heating the room. "I've got a bad feeling about this."

"Just keep working, and everything will turn out fine," Kirk said. He rolled over to Ross, and shook his partner's shoulder. "We're going to rule the world, and that loser will have to come up with a better threat."

"If you say so," Ross said. He pulled up the next file and went to work, ignoring the churning of his lower stomach.

CHAPTER 7

RUSSELL CARRIED EVERYONE'S bags onto the plane, including that of Armand and Duchess. He didn't mind; the weight was nothing. He could manage them all in one trip, and Duchess deserved a break from carting around Armand's stuff. She was strong, but she was still a lady. Russell's little Keeper glared at him and his bags, though, and it made the larger man smile knowing full well what the smaller man wanted.

Russell placed the luggage on the plane floor, and handed the computer bag he had snatched up back to Alfie. "It needs charge, yes?"

"You got it," Alfie said, unzipping the case. He pulled his slim laptop from the case and looked for the adaptor plug in the wall. The crystal glass on his side desk sparkled at him, full of water and the promise of drinking from fine dish ware. Alfie lifted it and took a sip while his laptop booted, no longer caring about it's monetary value. "So glad this plane has internet and power."

"That makes two of us," Armand said, ruffling the kid's hair as he walked by. He pulled a curtain out from a side door and proceeded to divide the plane in two. He poked his head through the space between the curtain and the wall, and grinned brightly at the other two. "And right now, I need to use it to check in with the boss with a proper report. Catch you darlings in a bit."

Russell and Alfie settled into their seats as the engine began to warm up. Their take off schedule was on time for a change, and the plane was moving forward in as little as ten minutes. Alfie spent this time checking his mail, and double checking the IP locations he'd grabbed during their last chat with the killers. *No*, Alfie thought. *The programmers*. Alfie closed his lid and settled into the seat. His brain was playing tricks on him, and that was the last thing he needed right now.

A loud beep came from Russell's back pocket. He glanced at his new cell phone to see a text from Sam. He had just read the message:

> I screwed up. Calm down Armand.

At the same time he heard a "He did what!" come from the other side of the curtain. Russell sighed *You idiot* to himself before standing and waiting for the inevitable explosion.

The explosion came in the form of an enraged Frenchman.

"Your partner is worthless, you know that?" Armand shouted, slamming the curtain to the side. His fists were clenched at his side for a full two seconds before he pointed at Russell's chest. "Absolutely, totally a worthless sack of flesh."

"What he do?" Russell asked, ignoring the beeps of his phone. He didn't need to check to know Sam was sending message after panicked message begging for protection, or for his burly partner to run interference.

"That idiot was supposed to take care of Bethany's partner! Sam said he knew where that little rat was hiding, and that he'd handle it. But apparently he was too busy with his porn site to double check his info." Armand smoothed his hair down, sucking in air through his teeth. Seething. "Turns out, her partner was in the room just on the other side of Bethany's. Intel caught him taking a car to Poland. We've been told to go hunt the little weasel down and eliminate him, or not bother coming home."

"When was Sam given order?" Russell asked, thinking if he'd gotten any hit orders this week. It was odd for one to be assigned something, and the other not. That was the whole point of having a partner. "I do not recall anything with Bethany on our plate."

"Same time I was given the go-ahead to bump my hit up a week. It was just a Keeper hit, so since you had your own little trip planned they didn't think to bother you with it." Armand took a seat in the chair across the cabin from Russell and Alfie. He lifted one of the crystal glasses and tasted it. He spit the contents out on the ground. "Someone get me a vodka!"

Russell sat back down and clicked through various messages of apologies and other random "Cover for me, big guy!" pleadings. As he predicted. Alfie stayed quiet through the proceedings and mumbled cursing of Armand. Russell rubbed his shoulder.

"A freaking Keeper hit. What a waste of my talent," Armand said, lifting his glass for the stewardess to fill. "Looks like your vendetta will have to wait, Ruskie."

"Not a Russian," Russell said absently, still glaring at his phone screen. He flipped through another few messages. "Though we agree this is waste of time."

Alfie shifted in his seat, leaning toward the plane wall. *Both* Russell and Armand looked ticked off. That wasn't good for the little computer programmer. "So, we're going to Poland now to kill this guy?"

"Yes," Russell said, shoving his phone back into his pocket without replying to Sam. He'd let his regular Keeper sweat. He had it coming, and Russell's sympathy reserves were dried out. He instead turned to his much more nervous and well behaved current Keeper. "Bethany's partner is young man named Jimmy Fall. Is ex-military, but no trouble. Will be quick."

"It better be," Armand mumbled into his glass, dreaming of beaches and resorts he could be visiting. "I've got better things to do with my time."

Alfie put his laptop away and shoved a pillow against the wall and reached for his blanket. If this trip had just gotten longer, he was going to get some sleep while he could. Alfie dropped his glasses on the middle table, and made a note to punch Sam the next time they saw each other for getting him into this mess. He closed his eyes, hoping to dream of pounding the man's smug face in and pulling the plug on his website for a day.

Alfie's sneakers squelched as he waded through the deep puddles of blood on the floor. Thick and sticky, the liquid clung to the soles of his shoes with every step. It splashed blots of red onto the hem of his khakis, and Alfie wished he hadn't worn a shirt under his polo. His own breath echoed in his ears, his entire body on fire from the heat and sweat pouring down his skin.

Mumbling in the distance, soft voices and muffled screaming, came in and out through static, like a radio station trying to change channels in the middle of nowhere with no reception. Those horror video games where the protagonist's radio would sound when enemies were near shot straight to the front of Alfie's memory.

But that wasn't quite right either.

Alfie hugged himself as he walked, the blood getting deeper and deeper as he sloshed through it. What was once at his ankles had risen to soak the pant legs of his knees. Alfie didn't know where he was, and nothing looked familiar. It was dark. He could hear laughter around him breaking free from the static in sharp pitches.

He wanted his computer bag.

He wanted his bed.

Alfie whined, rubbing his arms and whimpering when he stopped walking forward. The blood came up to his waist, soaking into the fabric of his pressed suit (Wait, why were his clothes so nice? When did he change?) and touch the end of his tie. The red liquid only came up to his waist, but his chest was covered in red as the blood seeped up through the fabric. Boiling, Alfie felt like a lobster in a pot.

Looked like one, too, as he trembled and stared at the heavy liquid hugging his arms. It clung like syrup, and dripped off in the same sticky rivulets.

Everything bathed Alfie in red. Red as far as the eye could see in the ocean of blood he stood in, to his clothes and even droplets of it dotted his glasses. There was so much everywhere and Alfie breathed heavier and heavier and—

He should turn around.

Head back to where it was still shallow and only his sneakers suffered.

He touched the tie around his neck; if he were even still wearing his sneakers.

Alfie backed up, struggling to shift and head the other direction in the blood as it congealed and thickened around him. A sticky paste, its color red and black sucked against him. Tugging and pulling against his every movement.

As he moved, a hand shot out of the blood, splashing his face with the hot liquid. The arm grabbed at his chest and dug its fingers into his shirt. The fist twisted, Alfie screamed. He shoved it off, but another reached up and pulled at his clothes from the side. More and more hands came up out of the red muck, the smell nauseating, and the laughter rang in his ears. Alfie wanted to cry and vomit and they just kept coming up more and more. All those hands and twisting fingers and—

"Wake."

Alfie jolted. The hand on his shoulder shook him hard enough to rattle his brain and hit his head against the hard part of the seat. Alfie swatted away the offending arm and grabbed at his shirt. His chest hurt under his rib cage, tight and compressed, and he felt slick with sweat and grime. Russell leaned over him, eyes and face stern. Alfie looked around the cabin, the pristine—*not red*—cabin. He took a heavy breath, and let go of his shirt. Armand snickered into a book, while Duchess watched him with large eyes just past Russell's shoulder on the other half of the room.

Alfie sat up straighter in his seat, shoving his blanket away from him. He patted down his clean shirt, and straightened the unfamiliar tie. He pulled at it, fixing it as best as he could without pulling it out and re-tying it. "Russell?"

"Nightmare," Russell said. He backed away a fraction when the man's breathing calmed and he settled upright in his seat. Russell rubbed the side of Alfie's arm. "Happens to all first few times."

Alfie tugged at his tie, fidgeting with the silky fabric. He couldn't remember what he had been dreaming about, just that it was bad. Had to be. Alfie looked at Russell, confused. "I was having a nightmare?"

"Yes, you shouted out." Russell gave the man his space and sat back in his chair across from him. He tapped the edge of the chair arm, feeling awkward. "Felt best to wake you."

"Your screaming is still exquisite, by the way," Armand said, flipping to the next page in his steamy French romance—the only kind of steamy romance there was. He tapped the table leg repeatedly. Alfie's nightmare had been a much needed perk to cheer Armand up after the unexpected and annoying addition to his schedule. Armand licked his finger and flicked to the next page. "Quite delightful."

Alfie pulled out his laptop and opened it up, wide awake and sleep not looking like it was going to come any time soon. He'd seen someone be ripped apart and murdered in more or less cold blood, and then had spätzle right afterward. They'd played tourist as a distraction, sure, but Alfie doubted that a night throwing up in a hotel was enough to block it all out.

Now they were on their way to murder someone else in cold blood. Of course Alfie was having nightmares. Screaming night terrors? Whatever he'd experienced was called, Alfie would be weird to *not* be having nightmares. Alfie's hands shook as he typed. Normal. This was normal. Nightmares were *normal.*

Alfie stared out the window at the clouds below on their way to Poland.

Nothing about this trip was normal.

Unlike with Bethany, the group was running blind when it came to finding the missing Jimmy Fall. Thanks to Sam's slip up, neither Russell nor Armand had any idea where the man had run off after his last sighting. However, Alfie quickly learned that didn't mean they were excused from finding him. He needed to be dead on someone's doorstop, and it needed to happen now. Thankfully, they did still have one sighting to go off, and they landed the plane back down in the airport nearest to where his taxi out of the country was last spotted.

But otherwise they didn't have much to go on.

Alfie leaned on his hand as the group powwowed around a table. He tapped his fingers repeatedly next to an empty plate and a full tea cup. The warm scent of the black tea calmed Alfie, and he concentrated on it instead of the stale air outside. The group settled somewhere in a city— again, Alfie made sure to *not* know where he was—and chose a local restaurant as their base of operations. They finished eating a little bit ago, and Russell and Armand delved into discussing possible tracking methods, while Duchess and Alfie sipped tea.

Their job in all this was to sit and "look pretty," as Armand had said. Alfie had to admit he was looking more dapper than he ever had in his life.

Alfie wore a light-blue button down shirt with khaki slacks and fancy brown shoes that probably cost more than his entire wardrobe at home. His ensemble was completed with a red vest and black tie, both silk and of the same high quality as the rest of his clothes. Alfie couldn't stop petting the tie with his thumb when people weren't looking. His wardrobe had offended more than Armand, it appeared. Because at some point, Alfie was hard-pressed to figure out when, Duchess had replaced everything in his duffle bag with new clothing. *Everything.* Alfie was stuck being fashionable, or naked.

Armand had laughed, claiming Alfie was Duchess' new dress-up doll when he saw the boy in the new outfit. He knew full well that the outfit was new, and that there were more outfits waiting. Armand pinched Alfie's cheek and grinned like it was the greatest joke in the world.

At least Duchess left Alfie's hair alone.

Alfie finished off his tea, and set the cup back down on the saucer. The two pieces of china clinked together, barely audible under the chatter from the other half of the table. Russell and Armand had been bickering for a good hour now, both coming up blank with a way to find Jimmy Fall save for flat out going door to door and grabbing people one at a time. That was much longer than Alfie had planned to dedicate to this trip.

Alfie sighed deeply, and turned his head across the street. He caught sight of a used electronics store that looked big enough, and tapped his finger once on the table. He glanced at the other two once before popping up from his seat. Alfie said, "I'll be right back."

Russell and Armand both stood from their seats the second Alfie left the table, but Duchess waved at them to sit back down. When Alfie crossed the street, Duchess kept close behind him at a fair distance. The boys sat back down, Armand amused and Russell far more reluctant to let his cute little charge out of his sight. Duchess chuckled silently into her hand. All of her boys were so cute!

Duchess followed Alfie into the electronics store, and spotted him hanging around in the adaptor section. In the few minutes he'd been in the store, Alfie already had a hefty looking box under his arm, and a packaged wall adaptor plug in his hand. Alfie nodded to himself and slipped the new toy into the stack of goods under his arms. When Alfie started to search his pockets for a wallet, Duchess intervened. Smiling pleasantly at his wide-eyed puppy-dog expression, she took the items and carried them to the main counter. Duchess put the items on the company traveler's card and carried it back outside to the restaurant.

Alfie trailed behind like the puppy he was, and Duchess had to bite her lip to stop from turning around and hugging him.

"What is that?" Russell said the second his charge sat back down and pulled over his purchases.

"Power adaptor." Alfie said.

Alfie ducked behind Russell to reach the outlet on the wall directly behind him. He plugged the adaptor in, followed by his computer cord. Alfie set his new machine up on the table, squatting next to Russell in lieu of pulling over a chair. He tugged a rectangular piece of equipment out of his shopping bag and snapped the end of one of the cords into the side of his computer. A few quick keystrokes later, and he was on an encrypted connection to the internet. Alfie typed, glad the restaurant was empty and that Russell and Armand had scared the owner into staying on the other side of the room.

"We got lucky having a place that well stocked," Alfie said. Russell poked the larger box, and Alfie pushed his hand away. "And that would be a satellite internet modem. Please don't touch it."

"For what?" Armand asked, looking over the piece of equipment. Unlike Russell, he was at least somewhat aware of electronics, but that didn't mean he knew why the new little Keeper had it.

"Getting this stupid job over with so I can hunt down those two idiot programmers who ripped off Russell and go home." Alfie said, pressing his lips together. This wasn't his idea of a good time, but he really just wanted to go home and those two weren't getting anywhere arguing. He pulled up a few well worn programs that had collected dust as of late, and began running background process to cover his tracks. "Jimmy Fall use any credit cards, or a cell phone, or anything else that's use would be stored in a database?"

"You can track him with one of those?" Armand asked. That was a common tactic to find people if you know what you were doing, but did Alfie qualify for that? Armand leaned his cheek into his hand, and tapped the side of his temple. "That seems a little out of the law for someone like you to know."

"It's not exactly legal, no, but I can do it, yes." Alfie shoved his glasses up his nose. He opened up a few new windows and began the long process of covering his tracks. Just because he could do it didn't mean he wanted to get caught. Alfie rolled his shoulder, and gave up on his squatting to pull over a chair. He sat on the edge to keep from knocking his cords out of the wall. "I'm more surprised you guys don't have someone who can do it, or have some cop on the payroll to do it for you."

"We do," Russell said. Alfie was proving to be much more useful than Sam on his best day. After all this trouble, Russell considered trading in. Sam would understand. Russell smiled, crossing his arms on the table. "Boss is angry and cut off our access."

"Well, then it's a good thing I'm here," Alfie said, typing. He glanced at the three criminals, and held his hand up. "So how about it, card, fake name? What? I need something to work with."

Armand clicked open his phone with a wicked grin, licking the front of his teeth. One quick phone call and some swooning later, Armand had gathered what he needed out of a weak willed voice at the other end. He clicked the phone off with a grin. "He's using an alias, James D. Spring, and has a card under the same name."

"Perfect."

Alfie got to work, and an hour later, they had the last location that Jimmy Fall had paid for something using the card. Duchess wrote down the address, and called for a taxi. While Armand and Russell collected the rest of their things and talked quick strategies, Alfie packed up his equipment and blocked them out.

This trip needed to end.

Armand leaned heavily on Alfie, his arm around the man's shoulder and fingers tapping on the edge of his vest. Russell and Duchess both rested against a wall, their arms crossed. They had huddled up in an alley way across the street from their target, who looked over his shoulder in every direction while trying to eat a plate of stew and potatoes. His brown hair was pulled down over his eyes, and his plain shirt and jeans were wrinkled even from this distance. The man's heel tapped up and down on the ground like he'd had too many cups of coffee in a single sitting.

Armand grinned into Alfie's ear, voice smooth as silk. "Color me impressed."

Alfie blushed, wringing his hands together and fighting the urge to worm away from the hot breath on the side of his face. Armand only squeezed his hold, lips too close to his temple. Alfie swallowed, clearing his throat a few times. "Let's just get this over with, okay?"

"Couldn't have said it better myself," Armand pushed away and skipped across the street with his hands in his pockets. He whistled as he strolled, not a care in the world. Out in the open. Like he wanted to be seen.

And seen he was.

Jimmy spotted Armand mid-bite of potato, and made a run for it. He shoved over his chair as he scrambled away from the table, knocking into another customer and a waiter a second later. Armand sped up his pace. Jimmy threw the plate of food at his well dressed pursuer, and made a dash for the corner street.

Russell was faster.

Alfie hit the wall alongside Duchess when Russell launched himself from the alleyway like a cheetah. Russell had passed Armand sprinting at a speed that dropped Alfie's blood pressure, and was on Fall in a matter of seconds. Before the nearest onlooker could scream, a head was snapped. The body dropped even faster than the twist of the man's neck between Russell's monstrous hands in a motion that looked so easy he must have practiced. Alfie's knees hit the pavement as those around them screamed and Fall's body continued to twitch on the ground.

Human beings shouldn't have been capable of that sort of strength.

People scattered out of Russell's way as he walked back to the ally, ignoring everyone around him. Duchess—*When had she left the alley!* Alfie yelled to himself—lifted the target's body over her shoulder in a fireman's carry, and followed Armand a few paces behind Russell. Alfie used the wall to drag himself to his feet as Russell stopped to stand over him.

Russell said, "Over with."

Alfie nodded, words escaping him. He stayed where he was on the wall, unsure if his legs would hold him. Russell took Alfie's arm, and dragged him along with the group. Alfie caught sight of Jimmy Fall, and tripped. Russell scooped Alfie up into a bridal hold, now carrying him as they ran. Fall's eyes were open, staring at nothing as the head bobbed up and down on Duchess' shoulder. They blinked. Alfie's stomach twisted into a knot, not completely sure if the man was dead or not.

Everything was happening too fast.

I did that, Alfie said to himself, clinging to Russell. That dead body was on his head. Russell had physically done it, but the guard dog couldn't have attacked if Alfie hadn't pointed him in the right direction.

Alfie rested on Russell's shoulder and wished they were back on the plane.

Alfie was a small man.

Physically weak, slim and soft.

Russell was a monster of muscle, bulky and strong. Hardened like stone.

When he had first met the blond, Alfie had thought that Russell could break him in half if he wanted to. Alfie had also thought he exaggerated those fears from nerves.

Alfie wished that were true.

Russell's muscles flexed as he cracked the neck in his grip as easily as twisting off a soda cap. A thing that shouldn't have been possible, but it snapped off all the same under Russell's grip. The limp body crumbled to the floor. Alfie grew sick. His stomach churned like a storm the longer he watched the rag doll body on the ground. He shook, reaching up to touch his own neck.

The spine was one of the strongest parts of the body. All that bone and muscle protecting such important nerves and pathways for life. It was hard to cut through. Hard to twist. Movies lied. Snapping a neck like that was just something in fiction. But—

"Is easy," Russell said, turning toward Alfie. He stepped over the body, brushing off the side of his arm. He flexed his arm, showing off the picture perfect lean muscles. They pulsed with heavy blood and veins under the skin. Pride dripped from Russell as he patted his bicep. "With muscle and practice."

Alfie shook his head and took steps backward as Russell approached him. There was a chill in his icy blue eyes, and an odd concentration on his face as he kept his gaze trained on Alfie.

"Also helps when the other is small and weak, yes?" Russell asked, watching.

"S-stay back," Alfie said, wincing when his back hit the wall. He moved to the side, but Russell stopped him with an arm. He was pinned. Just like when he was at Russell's computer desk and the larger man towered over him there, too. And when he'd been held. Russell could always hold him in place. Alfie's breath hitched. "Please, I just—"

Russell wrapped his fingers around Alfie's neck, his thumb over Alfie's artery and the rest of his fingers gently surrounding the skin under the collar of his shirt. His hand was warm, the skin rough against his own. Alfie swallowed, his Adam's apple brushing against Russell's hand.

"What, what are you going to do?"

"You did a good job," Russell said, rubbing his thumb up and down Alfie's neck. "Could not have done it without you."

"No," Alfie said, reaching up and pushing on Russell's arm. "No, please. I didn't mean to. I shouldn't have."

Russell's eyes narrowed, and his massage of Alfie's neck stopped. The fingers hovered there, resting deceptively gently on Alfie's neck. Russell's ached with hurt as he said, "You do not like helping me?"

"I'm sorry!" Alfie shouted, feeling his eyes water. He tugged on Russell's arm, begging it to leave his throat. "I didn't want anyone to die! I just wanted to go home."

"You don't want to stay with me?" Russell shouted, his voice thundering in Alfie's ears. Anger and hurt mixed together in a trigger temper.

"Please," Alfie choked. He dug his finger's into Russell's arm, the muscles as hard as rocks and unmoving as a mountain. "Let me go home. I can't do this any more."

"If you do not want to stay with me," Russell squeezed and lifted, raising Alfie off the ground. The boy kicked and squirmed, not a single motion able to phase the guard dog. Russell glared, a cold gaze that froze Alfie in his place. "Than you can join the others."

Alfie's breath caught in his throat as Russell tightened his grip, digging his thumb and fingers around and into Alfie's neck.

A snap.

"Wake," Russell said, shaking Alfie's shoulder as the boy whimpered and curled around his blanket. He flinched in a violent jerk, and his eyes locked on Russell. Alfie's eyes widened in a terror that stabbed at Russell's insides like Armand's knives. There were four seconds of silence before the young man crawled out of the seat and walked across the plane without an other word. He huddled up in a seat facing away from everyone and wrapped the blanket back around his shoulders.

Russell followed, standing over the young man who looked ten years younger with every tremble. "Alfie?"

The young programmer shook his head both ways and bit his lip. He didn't trust himself to speak.

The exchange did not go unnoticed by the other two passengers on the plane.

Duchess stared out the window, glancing over once in a while in attempts to watch while being discreet. Armand, for once, kept his mouth shut. The disturbed look on Russell's face was enough of a warning to stay out of it. Fear and terror, he loved. Crushed anguish at rejection? Not so much. Armand managed to bury himself in his erotica as Russell sat across from his little Keeper, and did his best to block out the room.

Alfie kept his eyes glued on the crystal glass on the desk, untouched and empty. Each cut edge of the various shapes carved into the surface with the same detail he admired when he first sat down. He threw his glasses on the table when Russell sat down across from him. Alfie covered his eyes with both his hands, slumping further down. This was the last conversation he wanted to have.

"Another nightmare?" Russell asked.

Alfie nodded, and Russell remained quiet, waiting for him to speak.

"I helped kill that man," Alfie said, dropping his hand back into the soft fabric of the blanket.

He pulled his knees up onto the seat, knowing he looked every inch like a small child but he didn't care. His nightmare was fuzzy and forgotten, but he could guess what it had been about. Or at least who this time. Alfie could still see Jimmy Fall's limp body as clear as when it had happened, and remembered how badly it smelled by the time they threw him in a suitcase in the plane's cargo.

Alfie dropped his head into his knees, knowing his voice was muffled. "I wanted to go home so badly that I went and found him so you could kill him faster. That man is dead, and it's my fault. Because I was inconvenienced, he's dead."

Russell leant back in his seat. His answer was calm and as soothing as he could make it. "Would have died, either way."

"No, he probably wouldn't have." Alfie sat up and looked Russell in the eye. He licked his lips and clung tighter to the blanket. "You guys probably never would have found him. Your boss said not to come home, but I really doubt he'd ditch two of his top men because of one loser Keeper who got away. It was a baseless threat if you two thought about it for even five minutes, and even I can see that. He's dead and it's *my fault.*

"I showed you were to go, and you went! And poof! The guy's dead." Alfie stood up and pulled at his hair, the blanket pooling around his feet on the floor. "It was just so easy. It makes me nauseous thinking about it, and the worst of it is I knew it was going to happen! I knew what would happen if I told you were to find this guy and I *still did it.* What's wrong with me? You snapped his neck like it was nothing!"

Russell sighed. "Quick and painless."

"You didn't even blink." Alfie collapsed back in his seat. He rubbed his hands in his lap. "Why is this so much worse than what Armand did to that girl?"

"You blame self, took part." Russell pulled himself up from his chair and sat down next to Alfie. The man had water in his eyes, and his breath was increasing. Russell laid his hand on the young man's head and rubbed his thumb over his temple. "Not your fault."

"But it is," Alfie said, voice choking. He sniffed and shook his head. "It really is."

Russell pulled Alfie into his chest and hugged his side. He rubbed the boy's arm, and squeezed. Before Alfie could protest, Russell snaked his arm around and knocked Alfie out with a light blood choke. "Get sleep."

Alfie collapsed into his arms, body limp, but breathing even. Russell brushed his hair out of his face. He was sure the boy would be angry about that when he awoke with a headache, but Alfie needed a dreamless rest right now. Russell blew out a quick breath, before lifting Alfie up out of the smaller seat.

"You really like him, don't you?" Armand said when Russell stretched the now unconscious Alfie out on the seat cushions into a more comfortable sleeping position. "You don't even baby Sam this much."

"He is good person." Russell covered him with a blanket, and checked his breathing to make sure it was regular. He stood, pursing his lips and sighing deeply. "Should not have brought."

"A useful guy like that? You definitely were right to bring him." Armand shook his head, and walked back to his seat. He winked at Russell, and shrugged before getting back into his chair. "He'll come around, you'll see."

Russell doubted it.

Alfie woke with a splitting headache, and an odd feeling of numbness. He was curled into a soft blanket stretched across the sheets, and there was a pillow under his head. Alfie shifted, and rubbed the back of his neck and looked down. Someone had taken his shoes off, and he felt a nudge on his shoulder. Alfie rubbed his eyes as he listened to the cabin; it was too quiet. He rolled over, and Russell removed his hand from Alfie's shoulder.

"We're in Lithuania. It is time to wake," Russell said. Alfie sat up, and rubbed his hair. He sighed, and moved the blanket out of the way.

"Where are we going, anyway?" Armand asked from across the room. He straightened his blue vest, and lined up the buttons perfectly with his collared shirt. He kept his voice light, a desperate attempt to lighten the morose mood from earlier. "You have an address or what? Alfie over there isn't the only one who wants to go home already."

"Alfie?" Russell asked, quiet as if he were scared he'd startle the poor programer. "Would you please?"

"Sure, why not?" Alfie said, a numbness in his voice that was unfamiliar but comforting at the same time. He reached over and dragged out his laptop to double check the coordinates of the programmer's IP address. He wrote it down, and left the plane with the others. He'd already helped kill one man, what was two more?

Alfie handed the slip of paper with the general area they were looking for and handed it to Russell. He pulled out his phone, and within an hour, they were on their way.

The car they rented from the airport worked well enough for their drive to the little town where their programmers were hiding out. Alfie narrowed the location down to a small strip of houses on the west side of the town, but IP addresses were far from accurate.

"Alright," Alfie said, standing in the middle of the street closest to his location. Armand had his hands in his pockets, looking bored and yet still suave while Duchess checked her make-up in a compact. Russell stood close, but not too close. Alfie rubbed under his nose. "There's a good bet they'll be in one of these houses, but I don't know which one."

Armand removed his shades with a quick flick, and placed them in his overcoat pocket. He smirked at the bag of goodies hanging over Russell's shoulder already knowing what was inside thanks to a little recon from his Duchess; someone was ready for a fun time. And with the way Alfie was messing with his emotions lately, Russell needed it.

And while Russell's idea of a fun time and Armand's were very different veins, this still would prove to be arousing. For Armand at least. Duchess had already replaced her compact for a book, prepared to wait it out while Russell played. Best of all, their little guide was looking smart in the latest outfit Duchess had chosen for him. Getting to look at a cutie like that was one benefit, but flirting with Alfie could wait.

Armand was ready to watch someone's legs get broken and things to go back to normal.

"How do we know which one?" Armand asked, strolling alongside Russell and his Keeper.

"Well, we could go door to door," Alfie shoved his glasses up on his face, pursing his lips. "But if these guys are serious, we should probably find a way that won't let them know we're coming.

"I got it," Alfie said, snapping his fingers.

Russell smiled when the boy trotted toward the back yards of the houses. *Smart boy.* He hefted his bag higher up on his shoulder, and followed. "Checking power meters?"

Alfie frowned, though it probably looked like more of a pout. "Yeah. How'd you know? I thought you weren't good with computers?"

"Big machines, big power." Russell said. He couldn't hold back the quirk of a smile as Armand started to laugh behind him. "Even I know big computer needs more power."

Alfie bit his lip to stop the laugh at Russell's proud expression. Alfie shook his head. Russell shouldn't be making him smile like that. Not after the past week. Not after last night. Alfie rubbed his face and said, "You got it. These guys have to be running a personal server or something to that degree to keep track of what they're doing and all those transactions. They'll be drawing at least three times the power of their neighbors."

"You heard," Russell said to Duchess and Armand. He waved his arm at the row of houses. "Check meters."

"Yes, sir, Ruskie, sir." Armand saluted, laughing at the desired curse mumbled under Russell's breath. He strolled over to the first house and noted the number on the meter for comparison. "Whatever you say, commander."

Twenty minutes later, Duchess used her thumb and forefinger to whistle loudly and draw her companions' attention. She pointed to a meter on a two story house in the middle of the row.

Alfie jogged up next to her and whistled. The number was quadruple the other houses they'd looked at so far. He looked over at Russell and Armand who had joined them. Alfie pointed at the meter with his thumb and shrugged. "I think it's safe to say this might be a good bet."

"Well that was easy," Armand said, voice low. He looked over the house, taking note of back exits and windows. Seemed like a small enough place. "Not that I'm complaining, but it seems a little quick."

"You will check?" Russell said, leaning over the boy's shoulder. The numbers on the small device whirled, the power being used up even now. Russell wanted there to be no mistake before they got started. "Make sure?"

"Depending on their security," Alfie said, tilting his head to the side, "I can know for sure after ten or fifteen minutes on their machines."

"Is settled," Russell said.

Russell headed around the side of the yard, his target the front door. He knew the others would follow. It was time to make good on his promise, and maybe let go of the newly added stress in his life.

No reason not to hit two birds with one stone.

CHAPTER 8

A KNOCK SOUNDED on their front door, heavy and rattling.

Ross jumped in his chair, the sudden sound shocking him awake. He rubbed his eyes, cursing Kirk and his sudden need to work around the clock. Their next project would be amazing, but that didn't mean they had to give up sleep for it! Ross grumbled, standing up from his seat. He rubbed the back of his neck with a yawn, lumbering toward the offending door on autopilot. The demanding knocking continued, urgent and with a ferocity behind it that made his head ache.

"So help me, if this is that neighbor girl again asking if we want her pastries," Ross said, rubbing the back of his neck.

"Just be nice, Ross." Kirk said, sipping his drink. Visitors weren't that common at this hour, but it was bound to happen from time to time when you lived in a friendly community. Kirk didn't mind as long as they brought food. He couldn't figure out what Ross had against them when he ate everything they brought like it was going out of style. "We like our neighbors, remember? Besides, she thinks you're cute."

"Yeah, yeah," Ross said. "And I think you confused me with you. It's you she thinks is cute."

Kirk snorted in reply and Ross opened the door, revealing a *huge* blond man with blue eyes so sharp he thought he might have been stabbed just looking at them. Ross gripped the door knob as best as he could through the sudden cold sweat. The man looked over his shoulder at Kirk, and then to his side.

Ross licked his lips, and asked, "C-can I help you?"

"One moment." Russell clamped a hand down on the man's shoulder. The man shivered under his touch, and Russell nodded in approval. He turned over his shoulder and said, "Your turn."

"Hey!" Ross shouted, when a small thin man in glasses with a laptop pushed by them and headed toward the back room. A man in a sharp suit followed him, wearing a smile that would have given the devil a run for his money. Ross pulled at the hand on his shoulder. "You can't go back th—"

Russell covered the man's mouth. Not for worry that he'd alert his partner, but because Russell didn't care to listen to his annoying protests. From Russell's initial glance, he only saw one other in the room, and Armand would be able to handle him with ease. As well as anyone else hiding who might cause Alfie harm, for that matter.

Kirk yelped when the intruder in the suit pulled him out of his chair and wrapped a hand around his mouth. No matter how he squirmed, he couldn't break free from the hold. Another stranger sat down in his chair and pulled up his terminal window and began executing commands. The man started to type and Kirk squirmed. *What's going on?*

Alfie disarmed any failsafes he could find on the computer before accessing the latest files in his programming texts. Alfie choked as he looked through the program in process on the machine. It was a *monster.* A real, true computer nightmare. Alfie stared as he scrolled through the code and—Stopped. He wasn't here for that. Alfie quickly looked away from the file mid-progress, and dug through the archived files for the specific one he was looking for.

The drafts and final copies of *FlowerMantis69* stared back at him in a folder labeled "My Baby." Alfie prayed for the man's soul and his own future nightmares as he swiveled in the chair to face Russell. He waved his hand at the computer and back at the two frightened men. "This is it. We're in the right place."

"Wonderful!" Armand said, tightening his grip on the dingy man he held. He petted the man's cheek, and grinned. "Isn't that great? You get to play with us!"

Russell entered the room, dragging the man's cohort with him. Alfie's sullen face and fidgeting hands told him everything he needed to know, but he re-confirmed anyway for both of their peace of mind. "Correct?"

Alfie nodded, stomach tightening. "No doubt."

"Good." Russell released his captive and shoved him toward Armand and the man's partner in crime.

Ross stumbled, and struggled to stand straight as he tripped back.

Upright, he turned to face each of the intruders in turn, whipping his head around. "What is going on here? Who are you people!"

Russell stood straight, dropping his bag to the ground. It landed with a *thud* and a clash of metal. The heavy objects hidden beneath the fabric rattled. Russell cracked his knuckles, one hand at a time as he looked over the two men. "You took my money. I find you."

All the blood in Ross' body dropped to his feet. Kirk sucked in a breath behind him.

Russell unzipped the top of his bag, and lifted a baton from its depths. He whipped it down, extending it to full length, the black compound ominous in his pale hand. He smacked it into the side of the plaster wall, sending a crack from impact all the way to the ceiling. Russell grabbed the collar of the nearest man's jacket, and pulled their faces close. "I break you."

CHAPTER 9

ALFIE SAT IN a second floor bedroom with Duchess, his laptop warm and comforting in his lap. The hacker's home was a modest building with three rooms downstairs including a foyer, and an open floor plan living room and kitchen, with two bedrooms upstairs in what was once an attic. Russell and Armand chose to stay downstairs, so Alfie escaped upstairs. Duchess joined him about thirty minutes afterwards, politely sitting a foot away from his perch on the bed.

She sat quietly with her eyes closed and her hands in her lap while Alfie distracted himself from the screaming downstairs by connecting to the local network in the building and exploring their digital landscape. The shouting, crying, thick thuds and smacks echoed up the stairs and through the thin wooden door. Alfie pretended it was someone's television tuned up too loud.

Or tried.

When that obviously failed to distract him, Alfie focused on his work. The network password was tough and protected by a nasty piece of malware, but Alfie wasn't some amateur. He'd proven that enough already on this trip. But at least he'd never used his skills to hurt anyone.

That's how you ended up in the situation as the two downstairs getting their legs broken.

Alfie flinched when he heard an elongated wail through the door. He leaned over the computer and typed faster, systematically erasing their hard drives, and back-ups, and back-ups of their back-ups. Kirk and Ross, the names he gathered from their mail sitting on the nightstand, may not have deserved to be beaten to death, but they weren't saints either. Their active project alone could devastate millions of people.

While what was going on downstairs was horrible in it's own right, there was no point in letting other people suffer, too.

A plate broke downstairs, Alfie jerked and bit his lip—a pair of headphones appeared.

Duchess handed the headset to the dazed programmer with a controlled smile, the ruby red lipstick she wore glistened.

"Thanks," Alfie said, taking the pair of thin, black headphones. They said "noise canceling" on the side, and he nearly sobbed in relief. Duchess grinned and shut her eyes, perfectly calm listening to the mutilation downstairs. She was quiet as a church mouse, and Alfie felt his curiosity rise. He'd never actually heard her say anything. Even in the hotel room when he'd heard her and Armand through the wall, all of the moaning, groaning and filthy talk came from Armand. Alfie cleared his throat, twisting the headphones in his hand. "Please don't take this the wrong way, but can you talk?"

Duchess shook her head, smiling. She pat her throat in emphasis. Duchess snapped her finger and waved for Alfie to hand her the computer. She opened up a text program when he handed the laptop over, and began to type:

> I have aphonia due to physical trauma to my
> vocal chords. Please don't ask for details.
> Your stomach might not be able to handle it.

"Noted," Alfie said. Duchess handed him the computer back, and rubbed the bottom of his knee. Alfie blushed, and loosened his tie. She scoffed, huffing out of her nose and leaned over. Alfie's heart stopped in his chest, when she straightened it back up for him, pink nails tapping on his skin. She then took the headphones out of his hand and thrust them on Alfie's head. He stared awkwardly for a moment, before she pushed at his chin and forced his face to look down at the computer screen. "Thanks."

Kirk could see bone coming from his leg, a sliver of white beneath fierce gushes of blood. Ross whimpered next to him, tied to a chair the same as him. He had at least two broken ribs, but at least none of him were visible.

Their brute attacker was standing still, tapping the baton against his leg. He looked like he was contemplating his next move, not that Kirk could think of anything more he could do. The monster had already shown off quite a bit, though his friend throwing out suggestions didn't help much. The man in the suit sucked on a lollypop in the corner, grinning like a loon at their suffering.

Kirk straightened in his seat, biting his lip until it bled to keep from crying out. Upright, he addressed the blond man. "Look, you made your point. You can have your money back! Heck, I'll double, no, triple it, if you just leave!"

The man's eyes narrowed, and his lip pulled back in a growl. He left his post of observing his handiwork to stalk closer to Kirk. *I screwed up.* The man backhanded Kirk hard enough to sound a crack through the room. He snarled into the blow like wild dog.

Russell grabbed the man's hair and yanked his head back. "You think this about money?"

Russell, hand still buried in the loud mouth's hair, turned and kicked the chair of the squat one. He yelled, hard enough that he would be heard seriously over Armand's laughter. "You think this about the money!"

Kirk sobbed. His voice was broken and it cracked as he asked, "Wh-what else would it be about!?"

"You stole from me." Russell felt his rage building with every inch. All of his anger from the phone call to his bank to Alfie shying away from him in fear surfaced. The thieves cowered before him. Russell needed this. He yanked the hair under his fingers, snapping the fool's neck back. "You stole from me like I am just another man!"

"What?" Ross asked, eyes dazed and locked onto the welt growing on the side of Kirk's face.

"I Russell Hopkins! I top rank mercenary and hit man." Russell grabbed the thin man's face by the chin and turned it. His fingers pressed into the blackened, bruised skin. Drool dripped from the man's mouth. "You steal from me like I am John Doe!"

Armand licked his rounded sucker, crossing his legs one over the other as he leant along the wall. He shifted slightly, trying to get more comfortable as heat pooled everywhere under his skin. Armand loved watching Russell work. The ever calm man hid a fierce beast that adored brutally. He could beat his prey for hours and hours with a raw viciousness that came straight from his core. Something you'd never know just meeting him off the street. Russell played, far less bloody than Armand's own work, but it was all still so very satisfying.

"You insulted his pride, you amateurs," Armand said, slipping one of his hands into his pockets.

"How were we supposed to know that!" Kirk yelled. This was out of control. He was half a day's work away from ruling the internet, and these guys showed up to ruin everything. He hurt, they were probably going to kill him and Ross, and this—It was a nightmare. "The program is automatic!"

Armand shrugged, sticking the lolly in the side of his mouth. The cherry flavor reminded him of Duchess' lipstick choice of the day. He pulled it out with a *pop*. "Rule one of professional crime: Know your target."

"What?" Kirk asked, the world spinning and his vision blurring from the growing bruise on his cheek.

Armand scoffed, digging his molars into the flesh of his candy. If not for Russell's passion, he would never have been entertained by such weaklings. Armand concentrated on Russell's still heated anger and the twisting rage on the bigger man's face as his hand moved deeper in his pocket. "You always make sure you know exactly who you're stealing from or bedding. You never know when they'll come after you with a crowbar or a shot gun."

Russell slammed the side of the chair with his baton.

Armand grinned, "Case in point."

The two men cowered beneath him, worthless worms. Russell flexed his arm and raised the baton over his head. He was tired of this talk. Russell had made his point, and he grew tired. One hit to the temple would be all that it took to end this trip. It was time for this to be over.

"Man, remind me to thank Alfie later," Armand said, proud his voice was even while his hand played through the fabric of his pants. "Can't remember the last time I've had such a good time on vacation."

Alfie.

Russell lowered the baton, and looked at the two sobbing men. Their eyes scrunched closed, ready and terrified of their deaths. He dropped his hand, letting the baton rest at his side. Russell rubbed between his eyes with his other hand.

Alfie had found these men for him.

94

"What're you waiting for?" Armand asked, his voice raising, his fingers clutching hard against himself. Russell was stalling. The *bastard*. "Come on, I want to finish."

"No," Russell said. He backed up a step and headed toward his things. He closed the baton, and tucked it away in his bag. Russell gathered the rest of his equipment, packing it all away. "Done."

"What?" Armand yelled, ripping his hand out of his pocket. He hissed, adjusting his pants and pushing off the wall. "All this and you're not even going to finish?"

"I am done," Russell said, heavily accenting each word. "Pack up. We go."

"No, no, no." Armand shoved the sucker into his mouth and pulled his knife from his other pocket. Russell was not going to play nice guy now after all this! Armand stalked over to the two men and flipped it open. "If you're not going to do it, I will."

Russell grabbed Armand's wrist and squeezed as he yanked it back and twisted. "Leave them be."

Armand winced, and bit his lip to stop from yelling. Russell's grip tightened further and yanked Armand's arm up, bruising his perfect skin. Russell twisted and Armand yelped, his sucker falling to the floor. It cracked on the wood, the tiny chips of candy sprinkling among the blood drops.

Armand had already forgotten what a brute Russell was when he got going, and he had just seen the man in action! Why did he always forget that Russell would just as easily turn on anyone else in the room without a Keeper around to distract him? Armand looked over at the infuriated face on his peer and relented. Normally, he'd know better than to attack a fellow high-profile assassin. But he was already drenched in bloodlust, and likely unsatisfied for not killing those two for whatever reason stopped him.

The Frenchman decided not to push his luck. He tried to smile, and shuffled awkwardly in place as he tried to calm down. "Whatever you say, Ruskie."

"Not a Russian," the blonde man answered as he dropped Armand to the floor. "Let us go."

"Yeah, go." Armand said. He smacked one of the two men on the cheek, wiping his hand off on his pants when it came back covered in tears. "Lucky you."

Duchess rose from her spot on the bed.

Alfie looked up from his computer as she moved away, pulling down his headphones. The action was practiced and automatic, as if she knew what the three seconds of silence downstairs meant. Duchess probably did. Alfie waved back when she gave a tiny finger wave goodbye and left the room clicking the door soundly behind her. Her heels tapped on the stairs, each step echoed by a wooden creak. Alfie sat alone for about ten minutes, wondering if this trip was finally over and he could get back to his normal life.

Well, as normal as life could be once he showed up at Sam's place and smashed a computer over the man's infuriating head. Alfie erased the last file on the machine downstairs, and ran a reformat on the drives. He'd take a hammer to them later, but for now, Alfie slapped the top of his laptop lid closed. He fell back on the bed, staring at the worn ceiling, listening for any sound downstairs.

Alfie turned his head when the door opened. Russell stepped inside, head bowed. Bits of blood were speckled on his jeans, but he was otherwise clean. Russell joined Alfie on the bed and fell back beside him. They lay side by side, staring at the ceiling. Russell sighed deeply, exhaling a heavy breath. Everything about him seemed utterly satisfied.

Alfie bit his lip as they continued on that way in silence. The sounds of shuffling and Armand complaining worked its way up the stairs and through the open door, lessening the tense atmosphere but not erasing it. Russell kept his eyes closed, and Alfie tried to stay still. The bigger man rolled over and threw an arm across Alfie, turning to cuddle against him. Or rather, cuddle over over him considering their difference in size. Russell's weight crushed him, and Alfie struggled to keep himself from suffocating. Russell didn't move after that and just breathed softly as he turned and hugged the smaller man closer until they were spooning.

Alfie turned his head toward the wall, and rubbed his hands together that were now trapped at his waist. "All done?"

"Yes." Russell reached up and rubbed Alfie's hair. "I broke their fingers, legs."

He paused, and Alfie waited not wanting to hear more, but knowing he would.

"But they live."

Alfie blinked once at the wall. He jerked his head to the side, his entire body following now lying facing Russell. Alfie knew his eyes were wide as he asked, "They're not dead?"

"No," Russell said, shifting his hold but not letting the younger man go. He tapped Alfie's waist with his index finger, smiling to himself. Sam always did say Russell was a cuddler. "I should have, but I reconsidered."

"Reconsidered what?"

"You."

Alfie froze, eyes meeting the cold blue eyes of a man who killed for a living. "What?"

"I kill people," Russell said. He put his chin on Alfie's head. He spoke slowly, trying to make his words match his thoughts. "Guilt is, not a thing I feel any longer for that. You, you are different. Not meant for this life."

Alfie breathed, listening intently.

"Armand, he kills. Duchess cleans. No guilt, either." Russell rested his cheek into Alfie's hair, listening to the young man's heart pound in his chest. "You, you lead me here. You found them for me."

"Yes?" Alfie whispered.

"You will blame yourself for their deaths. Same as Fall in Poland." Russell placed his hand on Alfie's head. "Feel guilty you chose to save yourself. More nightmares."

Alfie laid quietly, taking in the words as they washed over him.

"I like you, good friend. So I maim, not kill." Russell gave up and hugged the kid fully. He squeezed tightly, feeling Alfie's heartbeat against his own chest and warm skin against his own. "Do not feel guilty. Not for them. No more nightmares."

Alfie pushed back, glad that Russell allowed the escape from his iron grip, and sat up. He needed to breathe, and Russell was just so heavy. Alfie pressed his lips together, fidgeting in place. Russell rolled to lie on his back, crossing his arms over his waist. They sat in silence, breathing together in the quiet room. It was comfortable.

Alfie crossed his legs at the ankle, and smiled as his eyes watered. "Thanks."

"No problem." Russell stood in a single motion, pushing off the bed. The moment was over. He stretched his arms far over his head. "Ready to go home?"

"After one more thing," Alfie said, rubbing the side of his eyes to wipe away the water. He adjusted his glasses and looked up with a smirk. Alfie grinned wickedly up at Russell with a renewed source of energy. "Can I borrow your baton?"

Russell tilted his head, but nodded all the same.

"He's got a good arm," Armand said, leaning on Russell. He rubbed up against the man's muscular arm, making a right nuisance of himself. Russell sighed, but Armand grinned on anyway. "Look at that swing. You been giving him lessons, Ruskie?"

"No," Russell said, shoving Armand off of his person. The Frenchman chuckled, but took a step away. Although, Russell had to admit, he too was impressed with Alfie Knight's swing. "And, not a Russian."

"Oh man, just break my hands again!" Kirk moaned, tied to the kitchen chair. He hopped up trying to move the chair toward the man hurting his babies, but all he did was wobble in place. Kirk yelled, "Stop him! Please! This is too much!"

Ross agreed, tied on the other side of Kirk's chair, leaning on his knees and hands bound to the backside. He jerked with Kirk's movements. "You people have no souls!"

"You guys know this is the only way," Alfie said, grinning.

Sweat beaded on his brow, and his arms were exhausted, but Alfie couldn't remember the last time he felt this alive. He brought the baton down on the hard drive again, spreading bits and pieces of green motherboards and circuits across the room in a shower of broken electronics. He stomped on a loose piece, cracking it right in half. Alfie's lungs heaved, but he grinned all the same.

The only true way to destroy a hard drive was to decimate it. Erasing, and reformatting only did so much. Recovery would be child's play for these two. So Alfie gathered every computer and piece of electronic equipment in the building and dumped them in the center of their living room. Alfie then took the borrowed baton from a confused Russell and went to work.

Armand and Duchess chuckled at him in the background, and his big blond companion smiled just the tiniest crook of a smile, but they let him have at it. Alfie was merciless, letting every piece of frustration, nightmares and guilt he'd experienced over the past week out on the stupid equipment that started this entire mess in the first place. Every hit was a newfound sense of freedom welling up in Alfie's chest, and the hope that he could go back to normal when he got home. Alfie jammed the edge of the baton into one of the towers and laughed.

If this is how Russell felt every time he broke a leg, Alfie could see how the man could love his work.

"I don't know why you two are complaining. You don't know how good you've go it," Armand said, opening a small flat case. He popped a cigarette in his mouth, and snapped the case shut. Duchess lit the end for him with a slick, silver lighter, and a puff of smoke met Ross' face.

"Ruskie over there let you guys off easy." Armand waved his hand toward Russell, the bitter smoke making delicate patterns in the air. He tapped a bit of ash onto the ground. "Let alone what I would have done to you, isn't that right, Alfie?"

Alfie smashed a screen, flipping the baton in his hand to smash the base into a piece of glass from a monitor. "Right."

Kirk and Ross slumped together against the wooden back of the chair, defeated.

"That was fun, Mr. Knight," Armand said as they stepped off the plane, back home on American soil.

Armand grinned to himself as the kid ducked away from his hand when he reached over to ruffle his hair. He could forgive it just this once, after all, he did get to have a little bit of fun on this trip.

Russell's trouble makers were both still tied up in their house, as far as Russell and Alfie knew, their equipment smashed beyond repair. In truth, however, while Russell and Alfie gathered their things outside, Armand slit the two men's throats himself. It was quick, and while Armand was unable to give it the care he usually provided, the job got done. Honestly, the things Russell did to spare his Keeper's feelings. It was as adorable as it was irresponsible. It was a good thing he had good old Armand to look out for him.

And, thanks to a quick called in favor, not only was the place spotless, but they had also cleaned out every single one of their bank accounts and deposited the money into the main fund of their business. Armand licked his lips. And what Russell and Alfie didn't know, wouldn't hurt them. For either half. Armand hated to advertise his little charity projects anyway.

But, he wasn't done yet.

"Call me up anytime if you need something, kid," Armand said, pointing a finger at Alfie's face.

"I'll be sure to do that," Alfie said. He had absolutely no intention of ever contacting these people again, but it wouldn't hurt to play nice. Armand dropped his shades an inch, brown eyes mischievous. Alfie made it a step before Armand snaked his hand around Alfie's waist and dipped into his pockets. Armand snatched Alfie's phone and went to the contact screen to type in in his information, still leaning heavily on Alfie's shoulder. "Hey!"

"And I mean that. Absolutely anything, if you know what I mean. Not only are you adorable, but I happen to freelance on the side," Armand said, licking the corner of his lip. He tossed the phone back to the kid. "And now you've got my number."

"I'll keep that in mind." Alfie fumbled the phone, but managed to catch it before it hit the ground. Armand's number blinked up at him, the name in his address book labeled "Sexy." Alfie frowned at it, and hiked his computer bag up on his shoulder. That could have gone worse. He followed Armand the rest of the way down the stairs, and Alfie wondered if he could get away with deleting it.

"I mean it," Armand said. He grabbed Alfie's wrist before he could think of pressing any keys. He pulled his glasses to the tip of his nose and made eye contact. Alfie's eyes widened deliciously and he grinned thinking of all the fun things he could to do with, and for, this cute little Keeper of Russell's. Armand rubbed Alfie's knuckles with his thumb. "You call me first, understand, not Ruskie."

"Not a Russian," Russell answered automatically. He dumped everyone's luggage on the tarmac, and frowned at Armand.

"See? He's got no sense of humor," Armand said, casually letting go of Alfie's hand. He thumped his chest twice with his fist. "I'm much more fun, and I clearly have better taste in clothes than the both of you."

"Yes," Alfie nodded, taking a step away from Armand. He glanced down at the borrowed clothes, and wondered yet again where they came from. He picked the front of his shirt, and decided it was best not to ask. "Do you want me to return these?"

"Nah, they look good on you." Armand shrugged. He straightened his golden cufflinks and winked. "Besides, Duchess'll be upset if you don't like the clothes she picked out."

Duchess took that moment to lift Alfie's phone from his hand. She added her own number beneath Armand's, labeled a simple "Duchess" before pressing it firmly back in Alfie's hand. The kid looked at the little name and number like they didn't exist. She grinned, and shook her head at his amusing expression. Duchess she straightened the orange and blue tie she'd picked out for Alfie one last time before he could escape and return to his land of boring polos and khakis. He blushed at her touch, and Duchess couldn't help herself. She kissed Alfie on the side of his lip.

Armand laughed, "Guess that means you can call her any time, too."

"Right," Alfie squeaked, feeling his face turn the color of Duchess' lipstick. Petal pink. He clutched the phone in his hand like it might break. This was getting out of control. Alfie swallowed. "It was nice to meet you."

"*Au revoir*, Alfie Knight," Armand said, grabbing Duchess' arm and pulling her away. Any more affection and flirting and that kid was going to explode. As lovely as seeing his insides scattered everywhere would be, Armand was pretty fond of Russell's new little pet. "I'm sure we'll see each other very soon."

Alfie nodded and stuffed his phone in his pocket before someone else could grab it and add numbers he wasn't sure he should have. Russell tapped him on the shoulder, and Alfie realized that finally, *finally*, it was time to go home.

Russell grabbed his and Alfie's bags and headed to the black car on the right, while Armand and Duchess headed for the one on the left. Alfie tagged along with the large blond who started this disastrous trip while the other two disappeared behind the doors and drove off to their respective homes, job complete.

Alfie and Russell approached the waiting vehicle, both ready for the day to end.

The driver side door opened, and a tall figure stepped out. He pulled off his shades, and dropped his arms crossed on the roof of the car. He grinned, teeth white against his fake orange tan skin. His artificially yellow blond hair turned almost gold in the sun light.

"Russell! Alfie! You two have a fun trip?" The driver waved, casual and collected as a cucumber. "You remember to bring me a souvenir?"

Alfie dropped his bag on the cement, stalked over to Sam, and proceeded to punch the man in the side of the face with every inch of strength he had. Sam's head hit the top of the car, denting the metal. Sam fell onto the concrete, groaning and rolling over.

Russell walked over, and leaned over Sam. He hid his smile behind his hand before Sam could see it and look betrayed. Russell wasn't sure he could hide the shaking of his shoulders as he laughed, however.

Sam removed his broken sunglasses and looked up at his partner. "What did I do?"

Russell squat next to Sam's head and patted him on the shoulder, "Alfie learn well."

CHAPTER 10

ALFIE'S CELL PHONE, complete with three more numbers than it had originally after Russell snuck his own in, buzzed as he worked on a client's computer comfortably from his living room via remote connection. They had downloaded some adware bug, and Alfie was removing the last few bits of it from their machine. Alfie answered the phone without looking at the caller I.D., "Hello, this is Alfie."

"Alfie," he heard Russell say on the other side of the line. "I have question."

"Is your email not working, again?" He said, taking a bite out of a cookie next to him. Russell had taken to calling Alfie over Sam for his computer woes, and Alfie found he didn't mind too much. Russell was an okay guy when he wasn't killing people for the mob. And after a few unwanted texts from Armand and Duchess, he learned fairly quickly that getting those sorts of people out of your life wasn't as easy as a finished job. Alfie shoved the rest of the cookie in his mouth. "Your email provider is probably acting up, again, which is not on our end, remember?"

"No, no computer this time." Russell tapped something on the other side. Alfie could hear shuffling, and something knocking over. "Sam and I, we are going to bowling night in hour. Would you come?"

"Bowling?" Alfie asked, his hand stalling on the keyboard.

"Yes," Russell said, a touch too loudly. "We drink beer and throw things at pins. Great stress relief."

Alfie bid his client a goodbye on the chat, and disconnected everything one window at a time. He leaned back in his chair, drumming his fingers on the touchpad of his machine. "Like a buddy night or something?"

"Yes, buddy night." Russell said, sounding awkward as he said the unfamiliar words.

Friends with a serial killer. Alfie closed his laptop and shoved it in his bag. He stood from his chair, knocking into the desk. The crystal glasses from his plane trip that Russell had snuck out for him clinked together.

Alfie threw his bag over his shoulder, and headed out the door. He answered into the phone as he pulled his apartment door shut, "Why the heck not?"

Acknowledgements

To God be the glory forever, and ever, Amen.

As always: Thanks to God in the highest for the talent to write, and the push He gave to everyone who inspired me, helped me, and encouraged me. And of course, thanks be to God for giving us Jesus, who loves you & me.

At this particular moment: I want to thank my family and friends who have been endlessly supportive as I've come to make writing my full time career. In particular, the friends who beta read this book back when it was only a draft, and have reminded me that it should be put into print. Well, now it is! All thanks to you (and you know who you are)!

And of course, thank you to everyone who took the time to read and purchase this book. You're the best!

About The Author

Grey Liliy is a young woman who claims the East Coast of Virginia as her home. She enjoys anime, video games, movies, novels, and comics of just about any genre. Liliy has been drawing & writing a comic of her own since 2005, called *The Adventures of Wiglaf and Mordred,* which you can find at http://liliy.net/wam. Her debut novel, *Children of Hephaestus* was published in September 2012 and is available now.

www.ingramcontent.com/pod-product-compliance
Lightning Source LLC
Chambersburg PA
CBHW052141220626
47052CB00005B/1149